QUEENS OF RUIN

SELENA COLLINS

ENDLESS ROMANCE PUBLISHING

Published by Endless Romance Publishing

First Edition February 2024

ISBN 978-1-963671-01-8 (paperback)

ISBN 978-1-963671-00-1 (ebook)

SelenaCollins.com

When I wrote this book, I dedicated it to my husband.

"For Matthew, whose love and support never wavers."

Now, I dedicate it to his memory.

I love you.

Always.

CONTENTS

1

It was morning when Elaura watched the snow fall in swollen clumps onto a thick blanket of white outside the window. It would've been a wonderland to a girl in any other time, but Elaura wasn't a little girl any longer.

She walked through the maiden's barracks, her feet shuffling down the aisles between the bunk beds. Around her a dozen or so girls chattered excitedly, like little finches chittering as they flitted around one another. To them, today was a celebration, a day when they would begin the Opening Ceremony as girls and end it as women. It was a day when their assigned mates would be presented to them. Elaura watched the girls as they smoothed kohl liner over their eyelids and patted balmy rouge onto their cheeks and lips, blissfully unaware of the political machinations behind their celebration. The truth was, this ceremony was little more than an arranged marriage, ritualized to give it some symbolic meaning for those forced to endure it. Nothing more. Nothing special.

Her eyes locked with a girl who stood out from the rest. Her eyes were wide, her pupils dilated, and the flush that crept up her cheeks was bright without the addition of any rouge. Elaura wished she could offer some words of comfort to the poor girl, but she stayed silent and kept them for herself, however selfish that might be. Elaura pulled her gaze from eyes that too closely echoed her own feelings and looked at the clock.

It was time.

She clapped her hands loudly above her head. Though they were all the same age, her position in the royal household came with specific obligations. This year, their twenty-fifth, she would lead them from maidenhood into womanhood in their first step toward their ultimate goal: motherhood. The girls giggled and fussed over themselves one final time before they eventually fell in line and followed Elaura out of the building into the snow. Their belted tunics draped from shoulder to ankle, but the fabric was not thick enough to protect them from the cold. They shivered and rubbed their hands up and down their arms, hurrying down the street and across a giant courtyard.

The sky was gray with wispy clouds that formed

finger-like trails across the sky. Their ends came together and fell apart in ribbons above them. Around them, the snow twisted and turned in the air as the wind blew. Their footprints joined countless others shuffling as quickly as possible from one point to another. Elaura led them through a passageway flanked by two massive columns and finally into the blessed warmth of a church. It was the central building in the Temple Complex and the hub of all of their rituals, especially fertility rituals, of which there were many.

A woman dressed in a pristine white toga, nameless and known only as a Matchmaker, gestured for the group of women to follow her through a door on the right side of the cavernous room. Inside the receiving room, they sat along the curving perimeter of the room and anxiously waited to be taken into the adjoining chamber one by one. They'd prepared for this since they were young, and the anticipation was so palpable Elaura could hardly stand it. As a daughter of one of the ruling Queens, she had access to more than the propaganda taught to children of the City. The statistics on domestic violence, depression, suicide, and more were incredibly high, but so was the birth rate. In fact, it was the highest it had been since the plague that wiped out two-thirds of the women on earth and rendered nearly half of the men sterile.

But the birth rate... that was the number they

wanted you to hear. Births were on the rise—the selling point of a totalitarian monarchy, Elaura thought wryly. Because when you focus on healthy, happy babies in the wake of a plague, it's easier to forget about the problems within the society giving birth to them.

"Elaura," one Matchmaker said. She gestured for Elaura to come forward and pushed her briskly through the doorway.

Once inside, the door was closed behind her with a bang that echoed through the dim antechamber. On the far side of the room was an arrangement of seven throne chairs and seven Queens atop them, including her own mother dressed in her most elaborate toga. Upon their heads, the Queens wore crowns adorned with jewels that looked as if they were stars themselves plucked down from the heavens and set into the precious metal. Who knew? They could be. She stared at those star-like jewels and remembered the wishes she'd made on them as a child. Staring up at the night sky, she'd wished for all manner of things. Now, she wished she could love her mother as others loved theirs, but that would require a different mother altogether. For hers, all she could muster was cold obedience for an alien presence who largely ignored her.

The alien race of Queens, the Nurses, and the Matchmakers had all arrived at the end of the plague, a force bearing love, light, and hope. They'd helped the humans, sired children with them, and systematically taken control so quietly, so outwardly compassionately, that they now ruled them and had for forty years without so much as a drop of blood spilled in resistance. Or so they were taught.

A ring of Matchmakers moved to surround her and began chanting, their voices echoing in the dim room. One stepped forward and removed her maiden's tunic and the braided belt she wore. The simple cloth symbolized youth and humility, two qualities held in high-esteem by the Queens. Stripped naked, the Matchmakers closed in on her, tightening their circle around her, and pressed their hands over her womb, belly, and the soft mound between her legs. They closed their eyes, and the chanting grew in volume. The skin beneath their hands glowed. Green light filled the room, casting eerie shadows across their faces, and Elaura felt her body pulse with it.

"She is fertile!" a Matchmaker declared.

Another woman approached Elaura with a pile of cloth draped over her arms, and the two wrapped it about her. The cut of it was loose and fell down about her body in waves, leaving her arms bare and her feet covered. Elaura heard a door open behind her, and she knew from the shuffling of feet that they were leading her husbands-to-be into the room.

"One... two... three..." the women said together, their voices an ominous chant.

One of the Queens in the center throne stood and raised her arms toward Elaura. "Today you journey from maiden to woman and soon from woman to mother. Three knots for three husbands," the Queen said.

A Matchmaker stretched a long piece of tapered fabric across her back and wrapped the belt of cloth around her waist, tying knots at the hip with the tail of it. The men at her back moved into view in front of her. Fabric similar to hers draped their bodies, though their chests remained bare. All the men looked to be in their late twenties or thirties, not as dramatic a difference to her own twenty-five years as she'd feared, and they were well-muscled speci-mens. This wasn't particularly surprising. When your entire culture revolved around a race of alien Queens obsessed with reproducing in the name of restoring the population, your body became a temple, and they expected you to keep it in peak condition. Any less was simply unacceptable. Elaura noted that all the men wore the same stony expres-sion on their faces, and she wondered if they were as uncomfortable with this arrangement as she was. Or perhaps they were like many of the religious zealots living in this city and perfectly content.

Her gaze locked with the man on the far left, and she felt a subtle pull in the pit of her stomach. He was the tallest by several inches, his cheekbones high, nose long and straight, his hair a rich, chestnut brown, but his countenance was gentler than the rest. His skin looked as if it was naturally fair, yet had turned golden in the sun. Likely, his assigned occupation must keep him outdoors. His brows arched softly over eyes the color of clouds on a stormy day, but as beautiful as the color was, their sadness called to her, beckoning her to reach up and stroke the backs of her fingers down the side of his face. Touching before the completion of the rite was forbidden, of course, so she refrained. Not to mention, even possessed the gumption to do it, such a gesture would surely signal an interest in this marriage that she surely did not possess.

A movement from the man in the center drew her eyes away from the one on the left. He shifted uncomfortably as the Queen spoke about marriage and duty and the sacred laws of procreation. Clearly, the tradition of pod marriages was not one he was keen on. She wondered if he was old enough to remember the time before, when marriages were between two people alone. The dim light made his umber skin look damp and turned his dark eyes black, his brows furrowed over them. His jaw clenched tight, and his wide-set nose flared angrily. He never looked directly at her, only stared at a spot somewhere between her feet. She noted that unlike the longer styles worn by the other men, he kept his black hair closely shorn, and along his cheeks and jawline was a short, dense beard. She wondered what could've happened on his journey here to light such a fire of anger within him.

And what force of will kept it from roaring into a blaze?

The Matchmakers began chanting together, and the man on the right met her eyes and raised a brow at her, smirking. While the entire ritual frustrated her, it seemed it amused him more than anything. His dark brown hair fell in waves just past his shoulders, and his tawny skin glistened as the shadows and light played over it. His nose was straight, his chin and cheeks sharp and covered with a short, prickly beard. He reminded her of a pirate, or at least what imagined a pirate might be, though his hands were more like a pianist.

As the voices died down, each man stepped forward to untie one knot in her sash. Their skin smelled of wood smoke and ash, and they were so close that the heat poured in waves from their bodies. When the pirate-like man undid the last knot, he draped the loose cloth over her head and shoulders and took his place beside her. The other men did the same until they were all facing the Queens. The Matchmakers closed the circle in around them even tighter, and Elaura held her breath. This was when they would be pronounced a pod, a marital unit of one female and three males chosen by the Matchmakers and sent forth into the City to heal the world.

Elaura moved robotically as the rest of the ceremony passed in a blur. When it was over, a Nurse led them from the dim chamber through a winding corridor and into the bright light of the wintry outdoors. The icy wind instantly bit into her skin, and she pulled the mantle around her shoulders tighter. The Nurse hurried Elaura and her new husbands along to the family district where an apartment awaited them in one of a half dozen buildings. As they walked, Elaura daydreamed of the marriage ceremonies from the Before. Not that she really knew anything about them, but she liked to imagine. Did the couple say their vows or did someone preside over the ritual? Did they joyfully embrace or passionately kiss? Were they held in privacy inside temples or celebrated under the open sky? Such information was closely guarded, but she'd once seen pictures of women in long white gowns and men wearing tailored jackets with bows at their necks. It must have been beautiful. The start of a life, the promise of a happy tomorrow and tomorrow and tomorrow again.

Finally, they arrived at one of the family buildings and rode an elevator together up to the tenth floor. No one spoke, though she could hear their breathing, feel it on her neck. The Nurse showed them to a unit, number 1004, and ushered them inside. They'd traveled the entire distance without having ever passing another soul. The Nurse closed the door behind them with a smart click and proceeded directly into a brief tour of the apartment. She showed them through a kitchen, living space, a bedroom for each man, a communal bedroom with a larger than average bed, and, of course, a nursery. Notably missing was a private room for Elaura, for what could she possibly need with privacy when her sole purpose was breeding, she thought with a snort. The faster her husbands could impregnate her, the better.

Finally, the wholly necessary tour ended, and with a nod and a blessing, the Nurse quietly left. Elaura stood awkwardly in the living room, looking anywhere except her husbands who were casually milling about their new home.

"Better than the bachelor's quarters," the pirate said, and the stern one nodded.

The sad-eyed man turned to Elaura and said, "We should introduce ourselves then. I'm Gabriel." He gestured at the stern one and continued, "That's Talyn." Pointing at the one who smirked, he said, "And that's Orin." Orin gave her a lopsided grin at the sound of his name.

"That's your cue," Orin said when she didn't reply right away.

She cleared her throat. It seemed like it had been hours since she last spoke. "Elaura," she said. Her voice sounded like it had been rolled through gravel.

Gabriel reached out for her hand, cupping it and

bringing it to his lips. "We're pleased to be matched with you," he said.

Elaura pulled her hand away and into her chest. Her face was stony. There was so much she wanted to say, starting with how wrong this all was. Did they not know? Did they care? The frustrations she'd kept well hidden all day bubbled to the surface. She wanted more than to be relegated to life as a broodmare. Perhaps she didn't even want children. She didn't know. Not yet, at least. All she knew was this was not the life she wanted. Her list of objections went on, but there was nowhere to vent them, no one she could with such treasonous thoughts. Before she said something she could regret, she turned on her heel and left the bewildered men to stare at her back.

She retreated to the communal bedroom and closed the door behind her. Leaning back against the closed door with a sigh, she closed her eyes. She felt along the knob for a lock and realized with horror there was none. Her cheeks flushed in anger, and she beat her fists against her thighs. It was everything she could do not to scream! Hot tears prickled at the corners of her eyes, and her throat tightened. All her life she'd followed the rules, keeping her rebellions small and secret, always hoping she could somehow escape this fate. Yet still it had come to this. Still, she was forced into a marital pod that would never be a family.

A real family.

It was a concept that was foreign to her but held this mythological power in her mind. The idea of two people utterly devoted to each other and their offspring. Two humans in love, struggling and smiling, laughing and living together. A far cry from the cold duty that awaited her in this marriage.

Elaura smoothed her hands down her skirts, glancing quickly at the door as if to assure herself it was still closed, and took stock of the room. She noted that the room contained her writing desk, chair, and suitcase, and she assumed someone had moved them before her arrival. She was thankful that if she would not have a private space of her own, at least her belongings were here, though it was equally galling to realize that there was apparently never any concern that she would have said no to the marriage. It wasn't a surprise, though. No one did.

She wiped away the tears, now cold, that finally dropped onto her cheeks, and tossed the mantle from her shoulders onto the floor at her feet. She walked beside the bed, her hand trailing over the soft fabric as she worked to find calm and some semblance of acceptance.

Behind her, someone knocked on the door, and she turned to see Gabriel step inside the room. He was even more handsome in proper lighting. They all were really. She could only imagine how one of the other girls would've giggled and blushed becomingly at such a gift as were her husbands, but she could find no girlish joy in their beauty. This one's silky hair curled over his forehead and the nape of his neck, and despite her anger, again her fingers itched to touch him.

He moved closer to her, and she noticed the barest hint of a cleft in the center of his chin. How strange to feel such a pull toward a man she already hated. Well, to be fair, she didn't actually hate him, only what he represented.

"Elaura," he breathed. "I can't imagine that you're very pleased right now. Surely not every woman is jumping with joy on the day of her marriage, but I can promise you we would like to make you happy."

He stepped closer to her, and her eyes widened. Her breath caught as his hand slid over her hip, and he pulled her against him.

"I want to make you happy," he whispered.

2

Gabriel pulled her body against him, and the heat was so intense he thought he'd explode. She was soft and curvy, the flare of her hips dramatically meeting a delicious roundness at her belly. He moved his hands from her hips to the cord just under her bust and deftly untied it as she stared into his eyes. She was fascinating to look at. Her hair was an ashen blonde—long, thick, and braided up into the center of her head. It trailed behind her shoulders and down her back. He noted her skin was fair beneath his fingers as they explored the curves of her shoulders and arms, circling each dip and vein and tiny freckle as he did so. Her breathing hitched, and his lips curled in delight. He could almost hear her heart pounding out of her chest, and her pupils were so dilated that there was barely any blue left to see. He took his time about his exploration, watching for signs of interest or distress. While he'd been taught that it was his right and his duty to claim a wife as his own, the idea of violating a woman never sat right with him.

His hands bunched the fabric of her dress in his fists, and he closed the distance between their mouths until he was but a breath away. Her lips parted, and the air was heavy with anticipation. Slowly, he touched his lips to hers, and with one taste, she undid him. Her mouth was hesitant against his at first, but he doubted it was from inexperience. In their world, a baby was a blessing no matter how it came to be, and young women were encouraged to learn how to please men. Any pregnant unwed mothers simply found their path to the Opening Ceremony faster.

Boys were equally prepared for marital relations. Every boy's pubescent years focused on learning how to please women and men alike, a necessity considered the gender dynamics of marital pods. He was proud to say he'd taken his studies very seriously and was not ashamed to have enjoyed them.

But this. This he was unprepared for. This electricity between himself and his new wife was unlike anything he'd ever felt before. With every slide of lips against lips and tongue against tongue, he felt her relax into him. He pulled back for just a moment to draw her toga up and over her head, watching as it fell to the floor with a flutter of fabric at their feet, and revealed even more of her magnificence. Gabriel stroked the backs of his fingers down her high cheekbones, over her jaw, down the delicious line of neck, and over the heavy mound of her breasts. He cupped them with both hands, her nipples already hard with wanting, and leaned forward to press his forehead against hers.

"Do you want to keep going?" he asked. "It might kill me to stop now, but one word, and I will."

Elaura's swollen lips parted, her chest rising sharply with every rapid breath. He knew she was aroused, that she wanted him now as much as he wanted her, but he needed her to say it. He needed to hear the words.

"Please. More," she said, and her hands came up to wrap around his neck.

Gabriel groaned and kissed her again, his whole body responding to a sudden urgency roaring through his blood. He maneuvered her so that the backs of her knees pressed against the edge of the bed, then pushed her gently back down upon it. He knelt between her knees and slowly pushed them open. She sucked in a breath as he skimmed his hands up her thighs and to the softest folds between them. He drew his fingers around and through the soft curls of her pubic hair and then down through the center of her, slowly parting those lips to allow him full access to her.

"You are so beautiful, Elaura," he said, his mouth whispering up her leg from ankle to thigh as he spoke.

He kissed and nibbled and licked her soft skin until he was resting completely between her legs. He drew his tongue around the mound of her pussy and then down through the center. Up and around, he teased until he dipped his tongue into her warm opening. She cried out and pressed her pussy into his face as he moved upward and made slow, maddening circles around her clit with his tongue, his fingers pushing into her with long, languid strokes. Her hands streaked through his hair, and he relished how she pulled his head harder into her. She throbbed in his mouth, her hips pushing up to meet his face as he fell into a slow rhythm. He groaned as his face and fingers became slicked with moisture as he brought her closer to her orgasm.

When finally she cried out and shook beneath him, her body flushed and satisfied, he drew himself up from between her thighs and moved atop her. He guided his dick to her opening, rubbing it over her, though whether he was trying to tease her or himself was unclear. Inexorably slowly, enjoying every sopping inch of her, Gabriel pushed into her. She clenched rhythmically around him in the aftermath, as if trying to milk his climax from him. He withdrew and pushed into her again, then again and again, pressing his pelvis hard against her with every thrust. Waves of pleasure rippled over his body, tearing a groan from his throat as Elaura gasped and mewed beneath him. Her hands slid up his torso, her fingers dug into his back. He grunted at the intersection of pleasure and pain, fucking her faster, harder. His thumb circled her clit, still swollen and sensitive, until she was moaning again and arching up to meet him. He bent one knee up and pushed her leg back, reveling in her gasp as he drove even deeper into her.

"Oh my god," she moaned beneath him, her hands reaching up to fist in the blue satin sheets above her.

He watched as she cried out and felt her explode again, her pussy clenching around his dick as he pounded into her again and again and again. He couldn't hold back any longer. With a low grunt in the back of his throat, he slammed forward and poured into her, collapsing over her as he did so. He stayed still for what felt like an eternity, his heavy, ragged breaths ripping out of his chest in time with hers. The sweat from their brows mingled, and he silently wished for her to reach up and curl her fingers into his hair or stroke his back. He craved any touch from her, really, but he suspected she wasn't ready.

Gabriel pressed his lips to the side of her neck and then her cheek and finally her forehead. Stepping out of the lengths of fabric piled around his feet, he climbed up onto the bed and pulled her reluctant form to him, snuggling her to his chest. He moved an arm around and drew her circles on her shoulder with his thumb, listening as her breathing eventually slowed. She was still somewhat stiff beside him, but he knew it would be temporary. He had faith that they could bring her around.

"I take it that was satisfactory," he teased.

"It was," she agreed warily.

"We really do hope to make you happy," he said. He hoped his voice was sincere, though he suspected it wouldn't matter much if it was or not at this point.

She tipped her head up to look at him.

"We," she said.

"Mmm," he grunted. "Yes, we. I'm afraid there's not much we can do about that. For the good of the world and all."

"The good of the world," Elaura echoed.

He was silent for a moment, his fingers still toying with her shoulder. "What do you like to eat?" he asked suddenly.

She frowned at him, and he couldn't help but already love the way her brow furrowed. "Regular food?" she said with a breathy laugh.

"Why don't I make you something then?" he asked. "It must have been hours since you last ate."

"I'm not that hungry really," she said, but her stomach betrayed her and grumbled like the sorry traitor it was.

Gabriel arched a brow at her. "It seems someone disagrees with that," he said.

Elaura pushed herself up on her elbow. "Alright, yes, I'm hungry, but you don't need to make me anything. I'll take care of it," she said.

"It's really no trouble," he said and started to get up.

She was off the bed in an instant, putting her hands up as if to ward him off. "No, really," she said firmly. "I'll get it myself. I need a minute to process all of this, anyway." Her eyes then went soft and a little sad. "Please. It would be a great kindness to have a moment alone."

Gabriel nodded. He wasn't altogether sure what type of woman his wife was, but certainly anyone would need time to process the magnitude of it all.

"Okay," he said. "I'll wait here."

Elaura nodded and reached down to the floor to grab her toga. She tossed it around her body and fled the room, leaving Gabriel alone with his thoughts. His mind flashed through the events of the day and all the observations he'd made along the way. There was no shortage of them, that was for sure. Starting with just how gorgeous Elaura was. He had been careful not to create any expectations for how his wife would look. In truth, her appearance was fairly low on his priority list. However, he wasn't so holy that he didn't appreciate the beauty that she was. She was gorgeous, in fact, and only more so when he saw how responsive she was to him. It was clear their chemistry was already strong, but she was guarded and wary. He wondered why. Though honestly, as soon as he'd recognized her as one of the Queens daughters—her angular not-quite-completely-human features gave her away instantly—he'd believed she would be as spiritual as her sisters and brothers often were, as excited about the opportunity to fulfill her purpose as the rest of them.

Instead, she was obviously (and vocally) unhappy with the arrangement, and she did not try to hide her disdain for their pod. He only hoped he could convince her to make the best of it. It was the only way he figured he'd have a chance of tearing down some of those walls.

3

Elaura stepped out of the bedroom and let out a breath she hadn't realized she was holding. This was not how she thought her marriage would start, with blinding passion and mixed emotions. On one hand, her new husbands had worked hard to satisfy her, and she was more than satisfied if she was being honest with herself. She couldn't deny the glimmer of hope that there may be happiness to be found here. Hadn't that been exactly what Gabriel promised? On the other hand, though, an arranged married was still an arranged marriage, and she balked that the choice was stolen from her. Never mind that she'd known this would happen eventually or that it couldn't be undone now. Women, men, those in between, they all deserved the freedom to choose... whether that choice was who to marry or when to have children.

She walked to the kitchen and began rummaging through the cabinets, looking for a glass. From the corner of her eye, she saw Orin step into the room. He had a mischievous look in his eyes and his perpetual smirk on his face. He opened a cabinet on the far side of the room and handed her a glass tinted ocean blue. She took it without a word, turning her back toward the sink and putting her nose in the air pointedly. Unbothered, Orin propped an elbow against the counter.

"Why do you look at me like that?" she asked, filling up her glass with water and making a conscious effort not to look at him.

"Like what?" he asked.

She turned to face him then and took a sip of water. "Like you're about to take a bite out of me."

He pushed off the counter and closed the distance between them. His chest was still bare, but he'd changed out of his wrap and into breeches that laced up and should've tied at the center. Only his ties were undone—purposefully, she assumed—and the waistband of the pants rode low and loose on his hips. He leaned in close, so close that his breath whispered into her ear. She shivered despite herself.

"Maybe I want to," he whispered.

Suddenly, he pressed himself against her, and he scraped his teeth up the sides of her ear. He nipped the lobe playfully, and then his lips were sliding hot down her cheek. She fumbled the glass on the counter, nearly dropping it before grabbing his shoulders for support (or so she told herself). His dick was already hard and insistent as it pressed against her through the thin fabric of her toga, and she couldn't help but moan as he pushed his hips into her. Her senses went wild, her brain foggy and incapable of rational thought. She'd barely gotten her feet under her to walk in here in the first place, and now she was being pulled out to sea by a riptide masquerading as her husband.

He growled, his teeth at her ear again, grinding against her in a rough rhythm. It was almost painful, certainly somewhat unwanted, but there was something dark and delicious about that, and she felt her body responding to him.

Still wet and with the cum of another man dripping down her thighs, her flesh was already ready for him, and he was shamelessly taking advantage of it. He lifted her onto the counter, his lips crashing against hers with such force she was sure they'd be bruised the next day. He pushed her skirts up so that they pooled around her waist as his tongue dove into her mouth.

"I'll be damned if Gabriel is the only one who can take you over the edge," he said against her mouth.

Elaura was torn between intense arousal and the urge to fight against a man she barely knew taking her on the kitchen counter mere minutes after she was with a different man. Her brain was at war with her body, and in the end, she was simply too over-whelmed by all the sensations to do more than succumb to the pleasures her husbands were clearly so hell bent on providing. If there were any reasons she shouldn't, her brain couldn't seem to call them to mind.

If she was to accept her fate, didn't she want this marriage to work? Didn't she want to appease her husbands and find some semblance of happiness with them? Didn't she want a wedding night of body worship?

Her head fell back weakly as the pirate with the mischievous glint in his eye plundered her. Orin's hands were all over her, and then they were pushing her thighs even wider, his fingers diving into her. She arched against him, pressing herself into his hands as she matched his rhythm.

"Orin, I'm about to—" she panted, her orgasm so deliciously near.

"Not yet," he growled and tore his hands from her. He yanked his breeches down, and she watched in fascination as he sprang forth. He was of average length, for all her actually not-quite-so-limited expe-rience, but he was as thick as four of her fingers if she held them tightly together. Her eyes widened, and she felt like a virgin all over again, desperately worried it would not fit inside of her.

However, the worry was quickly replaced with

mind-numbing pleasure as he pushed into her and filled her to the point of bursting. He grunted as she took his entire length, gasping at the delightful invasion. When he moved in and out of her, her vision went black and she saw stars. She gripped his shoulders tighter, desperately clinging onto him as if her life literally depended on it, and when she reached climaxed, it rocked her like an earthquake. Orin drove into her roughly, his growls feral with need, his hands digging into her ass as he thrust again and again. With a roar, he slammed into her, pushing deeper than ever before and filling her with his hot cum as her swollen flesh throbbed around him. He dropped his head onto her shoulder, his breath heaving heavy and hot onto her skin. He pressed a kiss to the side of her neck.

"If this is a competition, I'm winning," he said with a grin.

Elaura couldn't help but laugh at that. "I need a shower," she said.

She scooted off the counter and turned her back to Orin. Before she could take another step, he grabbed her and whirled her around. A hand pressed against the small of her back until she was against him again, and his mouth descended on hers. He pushed his tongue into her mouth, stroking her there until he changed the angle of the kiss. Elaura felt her insides clench again as his hands moved to cup her breasts, pinching and rolling her nipples between his thumb and forefinger. He ground his hips against her, his dick already hard again. When she was thoroughly dazed and out of breath, he finally released her.

"That's so you don't forget me," he said casually, stepping around her and walking off toward the smaller bedrooms as if all he'd done was pecked her on the cheek.

Elaura stood frozen in the kitchen for several minutes, blinking her eyes in amazement. This was certainly not how she'd envisioned the day going, and she didn't know what to make of it anymore. One thing she was certain of, though, was that she did, in fact, desperately need a shower. Her skin was sticky with dried sweat, and the evidence of her husbands' carnal appetites was currently oozing down her inner thighs. She marched off to the shower feeling quite like a duck waddling across the room and decided it was going to be a long one. She needed time to think.

In the bathroom, she turned on the water and waited for it to warm. Stepping under the spray, she let it pulse over her hair and body and let her thoughts fall from her mind like so many droplets of water. The problem was, she thought, it was all happening too fast. She was adjusting to the idea of being married, trying to figure out exactly what that meant for her. Now, not one but two of her husbands were insistent on making her feel things she didn't want to feel. Worse, she didn't hate it or them. That surprised her the most. She was so staunchly against this arranged marriage, so against the practice, despite growing up in the Temple. How was she to build a happy marriage when part of her wanted to tear down the very structure of the society who forced her into it? How could those two things coexist?

She rubbed soap over her body and scrubbed away the residue of their lovemaking. If she could rid herself of the evidence, maybe she could pretend it wasn't an experience she wanted to repeat. Ever. Then maybe she could have enough space in her mind to figure out what to do about it.

4

The newlyweds fell into a tenuous peace as the days passed. One such day, they sat together on the oversize couch, watching the holoscreen. It was made from a clear glass rectangle that displayed everything from the weather to journalists announcing the latest news. Gabriel draped an arm over Elaura's shoulders, while Orin sat at her feet, casually stroking them as if it were not a conscious thought at all. As usual, it seemed, Talyn spread out elsewhere on the sectional. It was an arrangement that evolved fairly naturally.

Gabriel had become the de facto peacemaker of the group, and he had a gentle way of leading those around him without pushing. His priority was clearly to encourage them to become a pod in every sense of the word, friends within their family unit.

She liked him, and he was certainly the easiest to be relaxed with, but she was becoming more comfortable with Orin as well. She enjoyed his quick smile, and his clever wit made it easy to forget most days that they'd been forced together.

Talyn was a different story.

He was aloof, his manner curt, and he held himself apart in a way that confused Elaura. Why join in if only to hover at the perimeter? Even now, he was further away from the group than the rest. Gabriel supposed it was because he and Orin had known each other since childhood, while Talyn was brand new. He may feel out of place among men who were already closely bonded.

She didn't pretend to understand the secrets behind how the Queens chose the men for their pods or when, but she gathered they grouped the men together young to encourage bonding and a sense of brotherhood. She supposed that made it easier to manipulate them into agreeing to this ludicrous arrangement, though even she was having trouble staying so firmly against it.

In the days since the ceremony, she'd seen a side of her husbands that was wholly unexpected. While it wasn't the devoted partnership she once dreamed of having, Elaura found each of the men called to her differently. Gabriel was compassionate and caring, while Orin had a mischievous streak that was exciting. Talyn was still largely a mystery, but she caught him watching her now and again with a gaze that made her cheeks grow hot. Every time she met his stare, she wondered what might happen if that small spark of attraction fanned into a blaze. Would it burn them... or consume them?

A headline on the news blasted across the screen and interrupted her thoughts. The journalist's tone shifted noticeably, and instantly the lighthearted tone of the broadcast was gone.

"We interrupt this story for a breaking news report," the woman said. "Another brutal terrorist attack has occurred outside the Temple Complex. Early reports claim that terrorists have stolen as many as fifty cases of medical supplies and raided a fertility research laboratory. At least seventeen statues in and around the Temple Complex have been destroyed. There have been no reports of civilian deaths. However, three Nurses and one soldier were pronounced dead at the scene from injuries sustained during the attack. Another five soldiers have been hospitalized, and three remain in critical condition."

The screen changed from a view of the news studio to a camera panning across the Temple courtyard. A Queen, her tall humanoid form as breathtakingly beautiful as her size, stood behind a podium positioned in the center of the courtyard. She stared into the camera as it focused in on her.

"A full investigation of today's tragic events is

already under way. The terrorists have not only stolen valuable research, but they could very well have stolen the cure for the plague. I remind you that this plague decimated our world and continues to rob us of our future children. Our efforts hold it at bay, and they require constant vigilance on our part. The lawlessness and treachery of these terrorists has taken lives that cannot be replaced. We must stop these radicals at any cost. Our hearts are with the families who lost loved ones today. We will not rest until those responsible are punished," she said.

"Isn't it strange that she says 'our?' You'd think she'd use 'your' instead," Talyn said.

"What do you mean?" Elaura asked.

"She said 'our world.' Not 'your world,'" he clarified, his brows drawn together.

"Why do you think that's so strange? They've been here long enough. Wouldn't they consider this their world now?" Orin asked.

"If the Queens didn't arrive until *after* the plague, why say it decimated 'our world?' Wouldn't they say it decimated 'your' world? It would be the perfect opportunity to tell us how grateful we should be that they saved us," Talyn said, sitting forward and propping his forearms on his knees.

"It's possible she's trying to appeal to the masses," Gabriel considered.

"I think you're getting hung up on semantics. I doubt she even wrote that speech herself," Orin said.

Talyn shrugged and settled back into the cushions. "It's possible," he said simply.

Gabriel shot Talyn a look and slid his eyes pointedly at Elaura. It wasn't a look she missed, but something in her gut told her to pretend to, so she did.

"Remember," Gabriel said. "Speaking out against the Queens, even as theoretical questions, is still treason, brother."

Talyn fisted his hands, every muscle in his arms clenched, and it reminded Elaura of a loaded spring.

"And what good does speaking out do anyway?" he said hotly. "All that ever happens is talk. Decades later, and we're all still just talking."

Elaura leaned forward and put a hand on his thigh, trying to offer some level of comfort. He flinched. He looked down at her hand and back up at her with... was it disgust? Before she could work it out for sure, he stalked to his room, leaving Elaura confused and her pride smarting. That kind of treatment wasn't something she was prepared to stand for, not in her own home. There were probably a myriad of calm, emotionally mature ways she could handle this situation, but blind temper and bruised pride won out. She wasn't sure what she'd done, but she was already tired of walking on eggshells. More than that, she hadn't missed Gabriel's look, and she'd be damned if they considered her a sympathizer in her own home. Excusing herself from the group, she padded across the soft white carpet in the living room and down the short hallway to Talyn's room. She slid the pocket door open, stepped inside, and pushed it closed behind her.

"Go away," Talyn said.

"Tell me why you're upset," she said.

"I said, go away," he repeated, his back turned to her as he stared out his window.

"You know, you don't have to make our lives miserable. This wasn't my dream either, but that doesn't mean I'm not trying to make the best of it," she said.

"If you want a cookie for making lemonade out of lemons, you're wasting your time. I don't want any," he said. He crossed his arms over his chest to punctuate his statement.

"And what's so wrong with my lemonade, then?" she asked angrily.

"You're not making sense. Go away," he said.

Fuming now, it was everything Elaura could do not to scream and stomp her feet or, worse, commit some form of violence on this man's face!

"You're the one with the metaphors, Talyn. Why don't you tell me what you mean?!" she demanded.

"I don't know what you're talking about," he said, talking to her over his shoulder.

"Why do you hate me so much? What's the point of acting like you want to be a part of this if you're going to keep yourself at a distance?" she asked, the words tumbling out on top of one another.

Talyn sighed, and his head drooped. "Go away," he said.

"No."

"Go. Now."

"I said no."

"If you can't be mine and mine alone, I don't want you," he growled.

"Ah, so that's it. Well, we have something in common then. Not all of us dreamed of wedded bliss with a group of men. Some of us would've been happy with just one," she said.

Knowing she was walking on thin ice and depending more on her temper than her courage to get her through it, Elaura sat down on the corner of his bed. Talyn watched her cautiously.

"Did you know the daughters grow up in the Temple?" she asked after a moment of silence. "Of course you do, but most don't know that we rarely went anywhere else for fear of tainting us. Most of us dreamed of nothing more than ensuring that our husbands are handsome and kind, that we can bear healthy children. But my dream wasn't for a trio of handsome husbands and fat babies. My dream was to choose. Once, I begged my mother to change the laws, to let me choose one man to be with. I promised her I would still bear children, as many as she needed. I stared into the night sky every night, wishing the next day would be the one where we'd get that freedom. Then I grew up, and I learned wishes don't come true."

He uncrossed his arms and walked toward her. He sat down, and his expression was softer somehow. They sat together in stillness for many minutes.

"I had a woman once," he said finally, his voice barely a whisper. "Tall, willowy, black as night and just as beautiful, but sad. So sad. We were married— she and the husbands chosen for her—and escorted to this very building. A year after our ceremony, to the hour, we found her in the bath. She'd slit her wrists, and she was gone. Just like that."

"I'm so sorry."

"I never saw her smile. Not once. Do you know how red the water goes when that happens?"

Elaura shook her head.

His eyes looked across the room, but he wasn't really looking there. His gaze was far, far away in both time and place. "I'll never forget how that water looked. Or how ashen her face was in death. The autopsy revealed she was pregnant, though only just. None of us knew, but I think she did."

Elaura shook her head again. She reached a hand over and let it rest on his thigh, leaning into him and laying her head on his shoulder. It took a moment, but he relaxed and leaned his head into hers in return. "I can't replace what you lost. I wouldn't want to even if I could, but this is our family. It doesn't have to be a miserable one. I thought I didn't care. I thought I'd keep myself apart, but you've all started wriggling your way into my heart. Maybe we can't have the dream or love or wishes that come true, but partners? I think we can have that. Contentment? Maybe. But I can't build that bridge alone, and..."

Her voice broke as tears threatened.

"I'm afraid if I try to do it alone or pretend I don't want to at least try for some kind of happiness, I'll end up like your wife and all the others," she said.

Elaura turned to him then, tipping her face up to his. His jaw flexed, and his pulsed jumped at his throat. Without breaking his gaze, she gently crawled into his lap. She ran her hands up his chest, excited by the hard lines of muscles there. If growing up as a daughter of the Queens had taught her anything, it was how to use seduction to build bonds. Oh, she'd meant what she said. That was true. She didn't want to be miserable in her own home, and if coming to terms with this life and bonding with her husbands was what she needed to do to find some semblance of happiness, then so be it. More than that, though, he was hurting. Her husband was hurting, and she'd been taught a hundred ways in a dozen positions just how to use her body to ease that pain, even temporarily.

The sun cast a golden glow over his dark skin that made him look like a fierce warrior of the sun, but his gaze undid her. His dark eyes bore into her with such ferocity that it was a miracle she didn't combust.

He shook his head at her and said, "I can't share you."

"You'll learn," she said, locking her arms around his neck and using her teeth, lips, and tongue to tease up his neck. She moaned softly into his ear, grinding her hips against him. She smiled against his earlobe when his hands glided up her thighs, and he grabbed her ass.

"I don't want to," he whispered hoarsely.

"We don't always get what we want," she said seductively. "Or do we..."

Her lips moved to cover his, and he lost control. He growled against her mouth, pulling her roughly to him as she ground against him, stirred onward by the sensation of his hard shaft between her legs. Only thin pieces of fabric separated them, and she was sure to soak through them any moment if they didn't get them removed.

Dizzy with need, Talyn pushed down his waistband and shoved aside her undergarments. He ripped the draped top of her toga down and exposed her breasts, heavy and jutting out with need. His head dipped low to take one of her nipples in his mouth, pressing and circling it with his tongue, then suckling until she was panting against him. He raised her up and brought her down onto him, pushing into her in one swift movement. She gasped and cried out at the intrusion, rocking against him, and his entire body shook in an effort to keep from slamming into her again and again right then. He coaxed her on with his words. Faster, harder, yes, do it, just like that. His hands gripped her ass and propelling her forward and back forcefully. Her eyes locked with his, and he watched her climb, her cheeks flushing with exertion and arousal. Their bodies moved in unison, and when they came together, never once did they look away from one another.

5

As was their habit now, Elaura and Gabriel retired together after dinner. In bed, he tucked her into the curve of him before they fell asleep. Often Orin would join them in the night, sometimes snuggling into Gabriel and others into Elaura. On this night, Elaura woke in the middle of the night to find that all her husbands around her in the bed. Orin lay curled against Gabriel, the big spoon, so to speak. His hand draped low across Gabriel's belly, and their legs intertwined. While Talyn slept apart from the rest, she thought it was progress that he was at least present and curled toward her backside.

A wave of contentment washed over Elaura, and for a moment she considered maybe she was one of the lucky ones. It gave her hope that their marriage would be a pod who bonded, grew together, and raised a beautiful family. She smiled at the thought. Maybe one day she could enjoy motherhood after all. It was something to consider. If things continued to go well, she could be pregnant is as little as another month. Wasn't that the entire reason for assigning women to a pod? The more potentially viable seed filled her belly, the better the chances a baby would fill it not long after.

A vision of her heavily pregnant with a toddler and three husbands in tow played through her mind, and she thought about the playground that stood between the maiden's barracks and the Temple. When she was little, she used to watch moms and dads playing with their children. In her earliest memories, they were often just two people and a single child. If she remembered her history correctly, those were likely some of the last of the parents married before pod marriages had become law. For the good of genetics, of course. It was funny how quickly fear and sickness could make an entire population not only change their laws, but their entire society.

That said, with light there would always be dark. While she might view herself as one of the lucky ones, there were plenty who were not as lucky. Talyn's first wife was a prime example of the alarming number of suicides, all carefully covered up, of course. But nothing stayed secret forever. There were always whispers passed from person to person, rumors used simply as gossip or as fodder for more rebellious causes. How could a society treasure its women as mothers and yet show so little regard for their lives as human beings? It was enough to drive a woman crazy.

Or to action.

That was the pull Elaura knew well. She looked out the window and saw that the moon was full and rode high in the sky.

It was time.

Scooting out of bed, she padded over to her writing desk. She pulled open the middle drawer on the right side slowly, glancing at the bed to ensure her husband slept. Reaching into the drawer, she set aside the journals stacked inside and removed the false bottom. Under it, she grabbed a small pile of handwritten papers and carefully folded and sealed them, then slid them into the bodice of her toga. She tugged her corded belt tighter to prevent any of the papers from falling out. Grabbing the ceremonial mantle from a hook on the wall, she draped it over herself and pulled the hood down to hide her face.

She turned to creep from the room, only to discover Gabriel standing directly behind her. She yelped and instantly moved her hands to cover the papers hidden at her chest.

"What are you doing, Elaura?" he asked.

She knew he'd been sound asleep. She was sure of it—she'd checked and double checked, hadn't she? But his eyes did not look like the eyes of a man just out of a deep sleep. Instead, they were alert and zeroed in on her.

"I, um... well, the moon was so beautiful. I wanted to take a walk," she lied.

"There's a curfew. The terrorist attacks," he reminded her.

Elaura laughed and tightened her grip on her mantle. "Surely they'll make an exception for the daughter of a Queen," she said.

"I don't think so," he said.

He grabbed the mantle where she held it closed at her chest and moved to push it off her shoulders. As he did so, he pushed against her bodice and heard the crinkle of paper. His eyes flashed to hers, and before she could react, his hands grabbed the paper out of her garment. He quickly scanned the contents, and his mouth dropped open. Elaura sucked in a breath and closed her eyes, preparing for the full wrath of a disappointed father (or as much as she imagined one might be like) to be meted out against her.

"What is this?" he demanded curtly.

Behind him, Talyn and Orin woke and sat up slowly. Talyn eyed Elaura warily, but Orin seemed more amused than anything else. Because of course he was. Elaura said nothing, only glared at him. She refused to be made to answer to her husband as if she were a child, especially not about this.

Gabriel grabbed her shoulders and shook her, demanding once again to know what were the letters all about. Furious at being handled so roughly, Elaura crossed her arms and raised her chin defiantly. When he moved to shake her again, she grabbed his wrists.

Her voice was low and measured when she said, "Get your hands off me."

Her grip was firm enough to leave bruises when she wasn't careful, and he winced in pain. She *did* feel a little guilty for having hurt him, even if it was slight, but he'd put hands on her first. She released him, and Gabriel rubbed his wrists. He looked at her as if he was considering his next move in a game of chess. Elaura's mind raced, and she wondered what Gabriel would think about her letters. What would he assume? Would he turn her over to the authorities? Send her back to her mother? He could choose mercy, of course, but that was only if he was sympathetic to her cause. He could choose to exact the harshest punishment. The law would support him.

"What's going on?" Talyn asked.

Gabriel turned to his brothers. He gestured to Elaura with wrists already showing signs of bruising and held up her papers in the other.

"It appears our wife has a secret. This is a handwritten draft of the pamphlets the rebels have been distributing around the city. It's dated for later this week." He turned back to Elaura and remarked, "How odd that you should have such an advanced copy—and with a signature, too. Are you the '*People's Queen?*'"

She raised a brow and considered lying, but again, temper and pride won out over survival. "Yes," she said. "I am."

There was silence in the room, and Gabriel's face was unreadable. Now she would learn what awaited her. If her husbands turned her over to the authorities, they would no doubt torture her for information first before being given a traitor's death. Her half-breed status as a Queen's daughter would not protect her. In fact, it might make her sentence that much worse. It would be seen as the ultimate betrayal.

Orin was the one to break the silence.

"Oh, come on, Gabriel. Just tell her," he said. He ran a hand through the waves of his long hair and propped his cheek on the palm of his hand.

Talyn looked at him sharply. "We can't trust her," he said.

Orin shot a glance at Talyn and replied, "Clearly, someone higher than us already does."

"True," Gabriel agreed.

He turned to Elaura, who stared at them warily.

He looked as if he was about to reach for her, then hesitated and dropped his hands back to his sides. His bare chest heaved as he took a deep breath.

"Talyn, turn off the light," he said.

When it was dark, he reached into the pocket of his breeches and pulled out a small penlight. He clicked a button on its end and shined the purplish-blue light on his chest. At the hollow of his shoulder, just in the space between his arm and chest, a small mark glowed. The mark pulsed in the light. It comprised two short, vertical slashes that tapered at the bottom, with three small vertical dots that filled the space to the left of it.

"The rebel symbol?" Elaura asked, though it wasn't much of a question. She knew what it was. Rather, it was surprising to see it tattooed on the skin of her husband.

Gabriel nodded and shone the light on the chests of the other men. Each lit up with the same mark.

"The Queens can't see in black light, even when this glows, so we move in the shadows when we can and use what they can't see to our advantage. It's interesting that despite your bloodline, you can," he explained.

"But I don't have a mark like that," she said.

"You wouldn't," Gabriel said simply. "You have access to the Temple, to the royal household. Hell, you can even have private meetings with the Queen if you chose. You're too valuable to mark, and it's unnecessary. I'm sure only the highest ranks know your identity."

"And you three now," Elaura remarked. "What else don't I know?"

"About the rebels? I'm expect you're in the dark more than most. As much of an asset as you are, you're also the highest risk to the cause. If you ever defected, well..." his voice tapered off.

"Looks like we're in this fight together," Orin said with a grin.

"You *would* be enjoying this," Talyn said.

"Why shouldn't I be? Our woman is a fighter in the revolution, the *'People's Queen'* she calls herself.

"I didn't come up with the name," she grumbled.

"That's neither here nor there. It makes it even better. Who knew we'd one day have a Queen to fight alongside by day and ravish by night?!" Orin said.

He winked at her, and Elaura's cheeks flush with heat.

"I don't fight. Or do anything really. I only do the writing," she said.

Gabriel shook his head.

"The Queens have brainwashed the people of this city their entire lives into believing theirs is the better way, the only way. You call yourself a queen of the people and give them words that make them question everything they've been led to believe," he said.

"They're just words on paper. Making people question their lives doesn't make them ready to change them," she said, giving voice to frustrations held deep inside.

"Questions are the beginning."

6

The next morning, Orin gathered in the kitchen with the others. While there was a dining room off the side of the kitchen, none of them seemed very inclined to use it and preferred to eat here instead. Orin stood next to the stool where Elaura sat watching Gabriel scramble eggs in a bowl. It was the only noise in a room filled with heavy silence. The liquid hissed and sputtered when it hit the sizzling butter, and Elaura flinched as the eggs threw out a particularly violent pop.

From the corner of his eye, he saw Talyn standing with his back against the counter on the far side of the room, his arms crossed over his chest. He seemed reluctant, but it was clear he was trying to be a part of the family, more so every day. Still, he set himself apart and kept his thoughts to himself. Orin supposed he could spend time thinking about why if he was so inclined, but he was much more interested in Elaura's secret.

And secrets she had. One only had to look at her for a moment to see it. She sat rigid, her body pulled tight at every joint, and she held her head high. Though for all her bravado, she hid her hands in her lap and fiercely picked at the cuticles of her thumbnails.

Interesting, he thought.

"Where were you delivering those letters to?" he asked.

Her head jerked up, and she met his gaze in surprise, as if she wasn't expecting to hear him speak. She hesitated, and he figured she was deciding whether to trust him, or any of them, really. They may appear to be on the same side, but the Queens were canny with their spies and vicious if ever treachery was discovered.

"I was giving them to someone," she said cryptically.

He nodded. So that was how it was going to be. He turned his attention to Gabriel. "When is the next meeting?" he asked.

Gabriel didn't look up from the stove. He pushed around the scrambled eggs, reached down into the cabinet below, and set another pan to heat. He slipped sausages into the pan, shaking it briskly.

"I'm not sure," Gabriel said at last. "If they're

already getting the next letters ready, then I would expect it to be soon."

"And how long until it ends?" Talyn asked quietly. "Are we to continue throwing paper on the streets and raiding their supplies while our leaders hide from the real fight?"

"The Queens and their supporters are strong. The system is strong. Isn't it better to cut off the arms and legs first?" Gabriel asked.

"I'd prefer a well-aimed arrow to the heart," Talyn said fiercely.

"As would I," Orin chimed in. "But what about you, Elaura? What about your treasonous thoughts?"

He was goading her. He knew it. She knew it. But he needed to know she would not get them killed. He needed some show of faith that they could trust her, because there was more than just his life on the line now. Now his heart was, too.

"There are too many zealots to take the Queens head on, and they control the army. It makes more sense to weaken them before organizing a larger attack," Elaura said.

"True, and a surprisingly strategic opinion," he conceded. "But you have to admit, it's much less satisfying."

They lapsed into silence again, and Gabriel distributed the food onto individual plates. They ate together in relative silence, each of them lost in their thoughts. It was difficult to exist as one part of the entire fabric of a rebellion. You often ended up with all the rage of the whole, yet all the power of a single thread. It wasn't an existence Orin would tolerate forever, but for now he was less attached to that feeling of powerless than, say, Talyn.

When the meal ended, Gabriel and Talyn left to run various errands together. They were scraping the bottom of the pantry, and it was rumored there would be another food shortage soon. With no children born or even a confirmed pregnancy, they would be the last to receive food if rations were suddenly limited.

Orin volunteered himself and Elaura to clean the kitchen. They wiped down counters, filled the sink with warm, sudsy water, and fell into step as they worked their way through the chore. Orin hummed an old tune as he rinsed the plates under clean running water and handed them to Elaura to dry.

"Did you know they used to have machines to wash the dishes for you?" he asked suddenly.

Elaura nodded and smiled. "I've heard," she said.

"Why would you get rid of an invention like that?" he wondered aloud.

"Sharing domestic labor is an opportunity for bonding," Elaura parroted. She grinned and looked at him sideways. "Or so they say."

Orin laughed. He liked the way her face lit up when he teased her, and she decided to play along. It wasn't often she would, but he was hoping to fix that in time. She often held her lips, gently plump and sharp at every angle, pursed in attitude or disappointment or some other mysterious judgment against her husbands. It was sassy, and he wouldn't say he didn't like it, but he liked the way her mouth changed when she smiled more. It was a beautiful smile. Everything about her was beautiful, actually. Her nose was strong but straight and gently pointed at the end. Her almond-shaped eyes and cheekbones slanted up ever so slightly, likely the influence of her parentage, but he didn't hold that against her. Other than that (and her actual physical strength that exceeded the typical human), she bore little resemblance to the domineering Queens.

Today, she'd pulled the front of her hair into a loose braid that started at her forehead and curved over the back of her head. Tiny hairs escaped the braid, and he indulged in the urge to touch it, reaching out and pushing a lock back behind her ear.

Elaura looked at him, and his stomach clutched at the curiosity and heat that flashed in her eyes. He wondered if she felt this primal pull, too. Was she thinking about going to bed with him? Did she wish he was more like Gabriel or Talyn? Not that he cared so much, but he couldn't help his curiosity. She wasn't the most forthcoming with her thoughts, and their marriage certainly wasn't so mature as to make those feelings part of their everyday conversations. From what he observed, she seemed to prefer something from each of them and liked to keep her intimate lives with each separate. He may not like it, a pod should be whole and together in all ways to his thinking, but he was trying to respect it. Besides, he wasn't one to back down from a challenge.

"Do you remember the Before?" he asked.

Elaura shook her head and turned back to the sink. She picked up the pan he'd finishing washing and dried it slowly. "I was born after," she said. "I remember seeing the last of the Before couples, though. I'd spend hours some days watching them from my window as they played with their children at the park. When I was very young, they looked happy."

"But not later?" he prompted.

"Smiling faced turned worried at first, then they came less and less until not at all. I remember when they brought them for questioning, how the mothers screamed and fought, how the children cried, the way it echoed down the stone hallways. I didn't understand what was happening until I was older," she said sadly.

Orin nodded.

"Do you remember? The Before, I mean," she asked him.

Orin nodded carefully. "Yes, I remember. Most days I wish I didn't," he said. He took a breath, his eyes drawn downward and unfocused as if he stared into the past itself and not the floor. "I had two parents, two mothers actually. They were beautiful. One quiet as a mouse and the other fiery and exciting. If I try hard enough, I can almost remember what their voices sounded like or the way it felt when they brushed at the hair on my hair when I was up to something."

"What happened to them?" Elaura asked.

"Treason. They dragged us into the Temple, and I watched my mothers hang. They sent me to live with a pod family. I was told they would be a proper family," he said. His voice sounded distant and hollow to his ears, and he shrugged as if to push away the memory. Elaura's hand moved over his back in slow, comforting circles. He shook his hair out of his face, refusing to meet her sad eyes, and shamelessly changed the subject. "But enough of all that. What I want to know is how we get one of those dishwashers?"

7

Talyn was glad to see that the snowplows had cleared most of the snow away for his walk home. His knee-high boots crunched on what was newly fallen on the sidewalk, and he hunched his shoulders into his thick woolen cloak, tucking his hands deep into the fabric to stay warm. The sun was setting, and the wind was picking up as he entered the market square. Nurses walked from stall to stall, filling their baskets with produce, trinkets, and knickknacks for the children in their charge.

Most of the Nurses and some of the other women wore a toga similar to Elaura's. It was an oversize piece of fabric that draped down the body in waves. They wore it cinched with belts or cords at the waist, a heavier mantle thrown over their heads and shoulders to ward off the cold. Others dressed in styles left-over from the Before. Bulky sweaters, thick leggings, structured wool jackets, and calf or knee-high boots. It was odd to have such souvenirs existing so casually alongside a completely different culture, almost as if one painting was bleeding into another. He wondered when the practicality of allowing such outdated styles to continue to exist would be outweighed by the fascist desire to erase all but the present.

A vendor—she sold flowers from a hothouse out of a cart to his left—hailed him as he passed. Normally, he wouldn't bother even looking her way, but one flower caught his eye, and he detoured slightly to take a closer look. The petals were dark blue at the center and lightened to an almost icy blue at their pointed tips. Together they formed a fluted cup with a thick, bright green stem and long, pointed leaves.

"What's this?" he asked, gesturing to the strange flower.

"A Soulstar, sir," she said. She watched him patiently with folded arms and rocked back and forth on her toes.

He considered the flower, stroking a finger up the petal gently. "I've never seen one like it," he murmured.

"You wouldn't. It's a hybrid I bred from a tulip and a winter blooming plant brought here from the

Queens' planet. Would you like a bouquet?" the woman asked in a hopeful voice.

He didn't suppose the winter months were her most lucrative, yet food begged to be put on the table all the same, and the flower pulled at him. So Talyn nodded, and he exchanged a handful of gold coins for a spray of flowers wrapped in thick brown paper. He tucked them under his cloak and walked on. The Soulstars reminded him of Elaura, a hybrid herself and one that seemed to bloom in adversity. The nature of their marriage was still not an easy weight for him to carry, but he felt his connection to his wife deepen with each passing day, and that was enough for now. Never mind that he couldn't bear to open himself for more. That was tomorrow's problem.

There was a niggling fear in the back of his mind that when the government fell—and he hoped that future was not far away—she would choose just one husband to stand at her side, and how could he bear it if he fell in love and lost her, too? Better to avoid falling altogether. The thought didn't bring him much comfort, nor did it erase the fear, but he decided that was also a problem for tomorrow. Besides, it wasn't as if the rebels were hurrying anything along. It may be generations before they saw any meaningful change, and that was if they were even successful at all.

Suddenly, the hairs on the back of his neck stood up, and he risked a quick glance behind him as he turned to cross a street. Two men walked casually a few dozen paces back. It could be nothing, of course, but it was strange that he couldn't hear a single word of conversation between the two of them. Taking no chances, he made a sharp turn down an ally to his right. Another left around the back of a short, squat building. Alternate routes were his specialty, whether inside or outside the City. In fact, he spent most his day as a security engineer managing supply routes between the City and the various internment camps quietly kept outside it. There were countless routes, some genuine, others mapped out as red herrings, and they changed at random. Ordering himself to keep his pace slow and deliberate, his breathing normal, Talyn made two more turns. He moved another hundred feet and crossed the street. Finally, it seemed he walked alone again, though he wasn't confident enough to quicken his pace and risk attracting attention.

Once back outside his building, he pressed his back to the stone wall and took a moment to scan the street for anyone who seemed out of place. There weren't many who were out and about in this weather at this time of day, but those who did walk these streets moved with purpose. As he watched, he couldn't help but admire the last rays of sunlight slipping over the horizon. Those oranges and golds and pinks mixing in the sky were his favorite. Not that he would share that with anyone else, though. Finally satisfied no one was following him, he turned and went inside. He made his way up the elevator to their apartment, slid a clear rectangular card into the door to unlock it, and pushed inside.

Gabriel and Orin sat in the living room with Elaura having an animated conversation. Gabriel looked up as Talyn entered, and his face instantly sobered.

"What happened?" Gabriel asked.

Talyn hung his cloak, damp from melted snowflakes, on a hook on the wall and walked into the room. "I think I was being followed," he said. The bouquet hung upside down in his hand.

Elaura's brows drew together, and Gabriel leaned forward. "Do you know for sure? Did they follow you here?" he asked, his voice firmer than before.

Talyn shook his head.

"No, I can't be sure, but I lost them on the way," he said.

Gabriel nodded, and Orin murmured something under his breath, but Elaura shushed them. "There's no need to start that yet."

Turning to Talyn, she asked, "Now, what's that in your hand?"

He shook the mood off. She was right. There

wasn't anything to be had by worrying right now, not when he knew nothing for sure. He lifted his hand and presented the bouquet to Elaura. She slowly pressed her face into the flowers, cupping their petals so delicately as she inhaled deeply. He watched her savor them for just a moment, then moved the bouquet away and wound an arm around her lower back, gently pulling her to him. She tipped her face up with a smile, and he kissed her gently. Her lips were warm against his, and her body relaxed into him. He barely resisted the urge to nip her bottom lip and ravish her right there.

Instead, he said, "I have another present for you, too."

He moved to set the flowers aside and retrieve it, missing that Orin, ever the troublemaker, had risen from his place on the couch and was now behind Elaura. Orin grabbed her away from Talyn and spun her into his arms. Talyn watched incredulously as Orin did exactly what he'd just stopped himself from doing to her mouth mere moments ago. His stomach bunched into a knot of jealousy as he watched Elaura respond in kind. Temper flared in Talyn's eyes even as his body hardened at the sight. Blindsided by his own reaction, he channeled his surprise into more anger.

"Are you just going to sit there?" Talyn asked Gabriel incredulously.

Gabriel shrugged and wiggled deeper into the couch. He crossed his arms and said, "If you don't like it, you're welcome to do something about it."

Talyn furrowed his brows and glared at Orin and Elaura.

"Fine," he grumbled.

He jerked Elaura away, praising himself for not also slapping the smirk from Orin's face. Then he picked her up and threw her over his shoulder. She cried out in surprise, which he ignored, and carried her to his bedroom. The sounds of Orin chuckling and slowly clapping followed them until he kicked his door shut behind them and all was quiet. He dropped Elaura on his bed unceremoniously.

"What was that for?" she asked, angrily yanking her clothing back into place.

Her cheeks were flushed, and he couldn't exactly tell what emotions played over her face. Confusion, disappointment, curiosity. Arousal? Well, maybe not quite arousal. She actually looked fairly mutinous, and he'd never been more turned on by such a mood. He dug into his back pocket and pulled out a small, thin book with a stained plain cover and ragged pages.

"I wanted to give you your other present," he said. "Without an audience."

"You could've said that," Elaura said grumpily.

He simply shook his head. "It's my turn."

"I don't think Orin was thinking of a kiss in terms as childish as taking turns," she said.

"Mine," he said.

Elaura seemed to give up and shook her head in bewilderment. She reached up with both hands and took hold of the book he held out. She looked down at the cover and read the title, *A Maiden's Tale*. Her eyes widened, and she looked at him in surprise. The book was a banned book, though people in the right (or wrong depending on how you thought about it) circles knew and even discussed its contents.

It was a retelling of what the author remembered about an even older book long since destroyed by the Queens and their zealots. It told the story of a world where women became little more than breeders and their society revolved around bearing children. The fictional world depicted in the book wasn't too far from their reality, and many believed that was why it had been banned in the first place. Possessing such a forbidden book was treason, but Talyn suspected she would enjoy it anyway, and her happiness was worth the risk.

"Thank you. Truly, thank you," she said. "I'll treasure it. But you can't just throw me around whenever you want, you know."

"Yes, I can," he said, a fact he demonstrated by yanking her to him and turning them both so that he pressed her against the wall. Her pulsed leaped at her through, and her breasts heaved against his chest as her breath quickened. He remembered the way she'd looked with Orin, how her hands looked gripping him when he'd kissed her.

"Touch me," he demanded, grabbing her hands and pressing them to his hips. The book dropped to the floor, forgotten for the moment.

His mouth crushed down on hers, and she moaned against his mouth, opening for him and stroking her tongue along his. Her fingers were digging into his skin, and she was pushing her hips against his in frustrated arousal. Talyn reached down and pulled her knee up to open her for him, grinding his hard length against her through her clothing. Her breathing was ragged, but he wanted more. He moved his attention to her neck, and she arched against him, exposing more of her neck. His teeth nipped at the soft flesh.

"More," he said. His skin was on fire, and all he could think about was getting inside her. She yanked his loose linen shirt out of his pants, untied the cross of laces there, and pushed them down his hips. She grabbed his dick and stroked it as he whispered encouragingly in her ear.

With a growl, Talyn ripped her toga from her body and spun her body so that her breasts and belly pressed against the wall. He yanked her arms above her head and held them tight with one hand. She gasped and arched her back, pressing back into him invitingly. With his other hand, he grabbed his dick and used the head of it to tease her pussy until she was wet and panting with need.

"Please," she begged.

"Please what?" he demanded.

"Please fuck me," she said.

He leaned forward and clamped his teeth onto her shoulder, right at the base of her neck, slowly pressing his dick into her. Her pussy clenched around the head of him, and she strained to take more. He gripped her hip with his free hand to still her movements, his teeth tightening on her shoulder. She was dripping wet, her entire body rigid with need.

"You're mine," he said, holding himself just inside her, but no further.

"Ours," she argued with a moan.

"Mine," he growled, shoving his dick deep into her pussy in one swift motion. She gasped and pulled away from his length. He groaned in satisfaction, withdrew until he was nearly out of her body, and pushed into her even harder. Again he withdrew and again he pounded into her, and the sound that ripped from her throat was part groan, part scream.

"Ours," she repeated.

He growled again in reply, not knowing whether he was conceding to her or agreeing with her. All he knew now was that he needed to fuck her hard and fast right now until he was empty and spent. His mind slipped into that warm pool of pleasure where thoughts cease to exist, and his body took over until he was driving into her mindlessly. They climbed to the peak of where pleasure meets pain and, when it was almost too much to bear, cried out as they exploded together.

8

Several weeks later, Elaura snuggled into her bed with Gabriel, awake yet not quite ready to get out of bed. Orin and Talyn were already gone for the day, and Gabriel would make his way out of it soon enough, as well. While the bed seemed large and empty without them, she couldn't help but be a little glad for it. Her latest pamphlets needed to be less about exposing the system and more to motivate the people into action. Deliberate, violent action. She needed time with her thoughts, time away from her husbands. She wondered what would happen if they succeeded. Would her marriage survive it? Did she want it to? How much of her amicable feelings toward her husbands would stay if there was no longer anything forcing them to stay together? She didn't have any answers, simply contradictory thoughts and confused feelings.

And really, would any of it really matter when it came right down to it? Would she even survive this? It was one thing to be a person caught up in the revolts. It was quite another to be a Queen's daughter helping them.

Gabriel moved against her in sleep, tucking her deeper into him before his eyes fluttered open. She smiled at him.

"Good morning," he said sleepily. He rolled to his side and buried his head into her neck, his dick already hard against her thigh.

"Good morning to you, too," she said, wiggling just enough to tease him. Whatever may happen tomorrow or the next day or the next, she thought, she would not deny herself happiness or pleasure today.

Gabriel made a sound in his throat and playfully kissed her on the lips, cheek, neck, shoulder, breast, belly. He moved down her body slowly, his stormy eyes never leaving hers. His face was somber as he reached the soft curls of hair between her legs. He pushed her thighs apart, settling between them, and parted the hair and lips there until she was exposed to him. His tongue dipped into her in long, languid licks, and Elaura stretched under him like a cat. She grew wet from his attentions, her body flushed and delicious waves of heat began building in her center.

Suddenly, a loud knock at the door interrupted

his attentions, and Gabriel's attentions slowed. Elaura groaned. "No," she begged. "Let them go."

Gabriel smiled against her and rubbed his cheek against her inner thigh. "You know we can't. Stay here. Play," he said, grabbing her hand and pushing it over her pussy. "Keep yourself wet for me. I'll be right back."

Elaura sighed and rubbed her clit in lazy circles. She watched him pull on his breeches and, not bothering to tie them, pad across the bedroom carpet and into the next room. She heard the door open and a muffled conversation between Gabriel and a strange, feminine voice. The door closed again, and Gabriel walked back into the bedroom holding a square envelope. His face held no more of the easy playfulness of the morning, and Elaura pushed herself up on the bed. She pulled the blankets up to cover her breasts and grabbed the envelope he held out.

Elaura turned it over and saw that it was closed with a circle of hard wax, the Queens' seal pressed into it. Her hands shook slightly, and she couldn't explain why her heart raced or a stone formed in her belly. She slid a finger under the fold, pulled open the envelope, and slid out a piece of heavy paper, textured and yellow.

Her eyes passed over the words—words written in an ornate, flowing handwriting—twice before she took in their meaning.

Your presence is requested by your mother. Please

arrive promptly at the prescribed time below in the Temple's Receiving Room.

"What does it say?" Gabriel asked. He sat on the side of the bed beside her covered legs.

Elaura looked up from the letter. "It's my mother. She's asking to see me this morning. I wonder why," she said.

"Only one way to find out," he said.

LESS THAN AN HOUR LATER, Elaura was pulling on her toga and arranging the draping fabric over her torso. She tied a cord around her waist to secure it, wrapping her heavy mantle around her head and shoulders. Gabriel tucked it around her neck, more fussing at it than doing anything necessary, and kissed her forehead. They'd said little to one another since the letter came. There didn't seem to be anything more to say and nothing to be done but accept her summons. She tried to smile before she turned from her husband and walked out the door, but she wasn't sure if anything more than the corner of her mouth twitched. The door clicked shut behind her, and she hurried off down the hallway.

She wondered why her mother would summon her now. As a married woman now, she had none of the duties previously assigned to her when she was a daughter living in the Temple. Her only duty now was to produce a child, preferably more than one, and preferably as quickly as possible. Perhaps her mother was checking in on how her efforts were going? Didn't mothers do that kind of thing? She pushed open the doors of her building and stepped out into the City.

As she walked through the streets, she was reminded of the increase of rebel attacks—the media continued to call them terrorist attacks—recently. She could see the remnants of the recent destruction; it was quite a bit more extensive than what the news reports had shown. The rebels had chiseled stone signs off the sides of buildings, rubble littered a few street corners where statues once stood, and there were gaps in buildings boarded up with wood where glass had been. There even seemed to be more soldiers out on patrol. Perhaps this summons had something to do with the attacks, certainly not anything to do with her, but maybe her mother thought her time spent outside the Temple gave her access to additional information. Or perhaps it had nothing to do with the attacks or pregnancy and was about her marriage itself.

Elaura finally made her way into the Temple and down the various corridors that led to the Receiving Room. She took a breath and walked into the room without knocking. It wasn't expected. The room was lit with warm, golden light and arranged like an intimate sitting room. Shelves lined the walls and held statues, books written by the Queens or their various followers, crystals, and strange metal devices. Elaura always found it interesting how the Queens liked to blend items and styles and technology from their home world and this human one, even from various time periods. It made her wonder what their home had been like and why they left.

Her mother half-sat, half-lay on a chaise with a long toga wrapped around her body. Its folds flowed like water over her legs and to the floor. It didn't look like it by her current position, but Elaura knew that when she stood, she looked rather like one of the mythical Amazonian women from her childhood books. As Elaura entered, her mother raised an arm and gestured for her to take a seat across the room. There was a fire laid and crystal glasses filled with sparkling gold liquid.

"Elaura, how are you?" her mother asked.

Elaura sat on the chair across from her mother, her back stiff and straight. She felt awkward now, out of place. This place had never been comfortable, but it was once her childhood playground, and she'd felt like a part of it at least. Shifting in her seat, her fingers played in her skirts. The woman sitting across from her was almost a stranger to her. Queens bore many children but spent little time with any of them. To be the daughter of a Queen was to be a pawn, a tool of the monarchy, such as it was. Elaura wondered, as she did often as a child, why the

Queens looked so human and whether there was some cosmic connection to humanity. They had all the same governing features, and the differences seemed to lie more in proportion than anything else. Their stature was taller, of course, and other features like their cheekbones and brows and even the shapes of their eyes were simply a sharper version of the same features humans possessed.

"I'm well, Mother, as I hope you are," Elaura said.

Her mother made a purring sound of agreement in the back of her throat and smiled. "How are you enjoying married life? Have you conceived yet?" she asked.

"I don't think so," Elaura said.

"It's early still," her mother said with a dismissive wave of her hand.

Elaura nodded and clasped her hands together. "I suppose so," she said. For all her hatred for the Queens and her ambivalence toward her mother, the sting of rejection at her utter lack of concern for her daughter was still painful. Not that Elaura expected different.

"Have you met any of the other couples in your unit?" her mother asked, watching Elaura with a sharp gaze.

"No, I haven't. I've been..." she said, searching for the right words, "Busy getting acquainted with my husbands. We are hoping to start our family soon, of course."

The Queen's eyes softened, and her face relaxed. "That's lovely to hear," she said. "It's likely for the best. There was an incident involving the wife down the hall from you."

"An incident?" Elaura asked.

"Yes, she is no longer with us, I'm afraid. I don't know all the details, of course. I try not to trouble myself with such sad news, but I expect it was because of some complication from her pregnancy. She was carrying, poor thing, but as we all know, to bear the fruit of the world is both an honor and a risk," her mother said.

She was lying. Elaura *knew* she was lying.

Her mother continued, "The pod will have to be reassigned eventually, of course."

There was no way this death wasn't another suicide, another woman forced into a marriage to strangers to bear the burden of repopulating the earth. Her blood boiled at the thought of it. Looking at her own situation, she supposed she was one of the lucky ones. Her husbands cared for her, at least. There were others who were not so lucky. Men *were* taught to pleasure and care for their wives, but a Nurse had warned them once that violent thoughts from the Before were like an invasive weed, often killed but almost never fully eradicated. Despite the stigma against it (and likely because of the very nature of how women were traded like cattle), domestic violence and rape and abuse were still common. It shouldn't be like this. She shouldn't be sitting here considering herself "one of the lucky ones." A woman shouldn't have to hope for even a bare minimum of kindness or respect in her marriage.

Her mother cleared her throat delicately. She took a sip from the crystal cup in her hand. The golden liquid caught the firelight and shimmered as it swayed from side to side in the glass. With a small sound of pleasure, she swallowed and set the cup back on the table beside her.

"I'm sure you can understand how distraught the husbands are. Think of your own husbands and how they would feel if something were to happen to you. It's almost enough to drive one to tears, is it not?" she asked.

Elaura nodded warily.

"Of course you understand," the Queen cooed. "I knew you would. You have not been married so long, but still an attachment of sorts has formed."

"It has," Elaura murmured.

"Good. Now, it will be some time before the next Opening Ceremony, quite a long time for three young widowers to grieve alone. Perhaps you could go visit the men for the time being. Raise their spirits. You *do* want to start your family soon?" she asked, but it was clear there was only one answer expected.

Elaura's brows drew together. She nodded again. It was the only response she could think to give, certainly the only safe one. Once married, it wasn't customary for a married woman to visit a man who wasn't her husband, let alone a group of men. At least it wasn't to her knowledge, but something tickled the back of her mind. Why would her mother ask this of her? Why was it even necessary? It had to be something about the wife's death.

"Of course," she agreed. There really was no other option.

"Wonderful!" her mother said, clasping her hands together. "You know how men are, Elaura, how they have certain needs. I'm sure it will be a great comfort to them, and if you conceive that much quicker, it's only for the best."

Elaura's mouth went dry. A Nurse entered the room then and hastened to the Queen's side. She leaned forward, angling her body away from Elaura, and whispered something in her ear. Whatever she said had the Queen's gaze turning from relaxed to alert in an instant. The Nurse scurried out of the room, and the Queen turned Elaura with a too-bright smile. She gracefully slid her legs from the chair and stood, the long fabric falling around her.

"I'm afraid there are other responsibilities to which I must attend," her mother said. She stepped forward, reached out, and cupped Elaura's cheek with long, thin fingers. They were cold to the touch, her skin harder than a human's, as if it had pliancy or give. Then the Queen swept out of the room, leaving Elaura to make her way out of the complex alone.

Elaura kept her face a mask of obedience until she was well outside the walls of the Temple, but her anger seethed beneath the surface. Another wife was dead, by her own hand, like so many others. Yet all the Queen could care about was whether the husbands were being used to their full potential, whether they were actively breeding a woman regularly enough. Elaura knew this had nothing to do with their happiness or satisfaction. This was about producing children as quickly and efficiently as possible. It was about keeping the men not only compliant but enthusiastic about participating in the subjugation of women.

Because the more children who were born and indoctrinated into this society, the less power the rebels had. The Queens weren't rebuilding the population of the earth out of the kindness of their hearts.

They were building an army.

9

More than ever, Elaura was confident in her years ago decision to join the rebels. Although it surely had been impulsive, she'd done it for the right reasons. It was an interesting development that all three of her husbands were also members of the organization—high in the organization, it sounded like. She wondered if this special request from her mother meant that more husbands were joining the rebels. If so, it wasn't too farfetched to assume that keeping husbands pacified would be an even greater priority. Though that was assuming her suspicions about suicide were correct. In truth, the woman could've died any number of ways. Spousal violence or a traitor's death sentence were heavy contenders. Still, her initial assumption stuck as the most likely.

Whatever the reason for the Queen's "special assignment" for her, rebel numbers were almost certainly growing, a good sign to be sure, but it complicated matters slightly. As much as she and her husbands were united, she was still afraid of what would happen if they ever overthrew the Queens. Not for the world at large, of course. That was surely a positive. But what would it mean for them, for the family she was building? She and her husbands were still so separate, more like three separate marriages under one roof. Elaura wasn't sure how to bring them together or if she even wanted to. When she was with one of her husbands, he was the only one she was thinking of. It was almost enough to believe she had her fantasy marriage, a devoted husband to whom she was equally devoted. Him and him alone. In her mind, she could keep them each in their own boxes, together but separate.

But the more she tried to convince herself she wanted to do that forever, the more she missed the togetherness that was growing between them as a pod. It was more than sharing a home or meals together. It was the little moments that happened between them. It was the way Gabriel smiled when Orin kissed her or the warm feeling in her belly when Talyn and Orin joked with each other. It was the brotherhood that was forming between her husbands even as they become her lovers and friends.

She wondered if that sense of unity was something she would want in a new society, because if they weren't a unit before the fall, they'd never be one in the ruins.

She continued to ponder it throughout the rest of the afternoon and well into the evening. She couldn't imagine what life would be like if the rebels had their way. This was the only life she'd ever known. True, she'd seen pictures of the Before, but it was strange. Her world was such a mix of the old and the new, as if the Queens had arrived and done away with the existing power structures that would threaten their autocracy, but hadn't much considered the remnants of the various cultures left behind. You could see it in the melting pot of fashions worn by the people of the City, styles completely divorced from the culture they'd come from, or visit a home that boasted a holographic video screen but no automatic dishwasher. There didn't seem to be a strict rhyme or reason to it.

When her mind was exhausted and her eyes heavy, Elaura walked to the bedroom with Gabriel. He put his arm around her and led her to the bed. They laid down, and he pulled her in close in a now familiar gesture. She snuggled in and made a small noise of contentment in the back of her throat as he began gently stroking her arm in small circles. She heard footsteps at the door and looked up to see Orin walking into the room. He mindlessly ran a hand through his long waves of hair, scratching some itch on the side of his head, and caught her eye. He gave her a one-sided grin that had her stomach doing flips and moved to adjust the lamp light to just the ambiance she liked best. Who knew that someone remembering your lighting preferences could be so romantic?

Orin's beard was cut close, and her fingers itched to touch it. He slid into the bed opposite from Gabriel and snuggled in close. She liked the way his beard scratched against her neck, how his hot breath pulsed over her. Her skin prickled, her body growing hot in anticipation, and her lips parted in invitation. A breathy sigh escaped as his fingers, laced with Gabriel's on her hip, dig into the skin there, and he kissed her deeply. He knew how to take his time with it, building her up bit by excruciating bit. His lips moved over her gently, coaxing her open so that he could stroke her tongue with his. Gabriel moved behind her, and she shivered when his lips moved hot against her neck.

The first night of this marriage flashed through her mind, a time so recent and yet so long ago. It had been this, this physical act of devotion, that sparked the bonds she was building with her husbands. As much as she worried about their future, she also desperately wanted to be loved. For the first time in her life, she thought she could be. Perhaps it was this that would finally give her that and bring them all together.

Inspired, Elaura disengaged herself from Orin and Gabriel, despite their protests. She held up a finger, begging them to wait a moment, and hurried from the room. She walked through the living room and down the short hallway to Talyn's room. Outside his door, she hesitated. If her plan worked, this could very well lead to a depth of emotion that could jeopardize all of their hard work. How would it look for a group of rebels to help bring down the government and then still fight to maintain their marital unit? Though, she reminded herself, they weren't really fighting for the abolition of pod marriages. Rather, they were fighting for choice.

Hoping Talyn wasn't already sleeping, she raised her hand to knock on his door, but before her fist touched the wood, it slid open as if he'd been waiting for her. His dark eyes narrowed to slits, and he raised a brow. He turned slightly to allow her to enter, but she shook her head instead. Taking her hand in his, she led him across the apartment to the communal bedroom. Orin and Gabriel were both laid on their sides, talking in low voices when she and Talyn walked into the room. They looked up, and Gabriel smiled. Orin appeared skeptical, a brow raised, but he opened his arms in a welcome gesture.

Turning around, Elaura pulled Talyn closer to her, twining her arms around his neck and pressing her lips to his. They were full and soft against hers. She hummed with satisfaction when his arms come around her, and he fell into the kiss. He groaned as her fingers played with the coarse hair at the nape of his neck. She pushed their bodies around and forward until the bed was behind him and the backs of his knees knocked against it. Not so gently, she shoved him down onto his back. He scooted back until he was in the center of the bed, and Elaura crawled up to straddle him. Talyn jerked slightly when Gabriel pulled his shirt up and over his head, and Elaura pressed a finger to his lips.

"Please stay," she said. "Trust me."

Gabriel and Orin moved in unison to kneel beside her, but her eyes stayed locked with Talyn. Orin's head dipped into the space beneath her jaw, and his teeth nipped at the sensitive skin there. His hand snaked up her thigh and into the center of her. He rubbed her clit in slow circles until she was panting and pushing against his hand. At the same time, Gabriel's hand pressed against the small of her back while his other worked at her breast, cupping the fullness of her and gently stroking her nipple, rolling it between his fingers, pinching and pulling at it. Between her legs, Talyn's arousal strained against her from inside the breeches he still wore. She moved her hips slowly against him to the rhythm of Orin's petting, her juices soaking the fabric between them. With a growl, Talyn tore himself free of his breeches and grabbed her hips. He raised Elaura up and brought her down the full length of his dick. She was sopping wet, more than ready for him.

Elaura gasped and arched her back, rocking against Talyn and letting the sensations of Gabriel and Orin's ministrations pulse over her body. From every angle, her body was assaulted, the ripples of pleasure building into waves with no clear starting point and only one possible end. Her orgasm was sudden and powerful, and she cried out with the force of it. It pulsed from her center so powerfully that she tingled from the tips of her fingers to her toes. It sapped the strength from her, and she sagged against Gabriel and Orin as Talyn supported her hips and moved beneath her.

Gabriel captured her mouth in his and languidly kissed her, his lips moving over hers with practiced skill. As he did, Orin leaned forward and took Gabriel's dick into his own mouth. Gabriel moaned against her lips, breaking from them with a gasp and leaning his forehead against hers as Orin worked. He drew in a shaky breath and leaned his head back. Elaura watched in fascination as Orin moved his mouth up and down the length of Gabriel, all the while Talyn pounded into her from below, his eyes hungrily watching Gabriel's dick slip deep into Orin's mouth even as his dick disappeared deep inside of Elaura. With a cry, he emptied himself into her, thrusting hard and deep one last time.

Orin and Gabriel separated, and Orin moved behind Elaura. She leaned forward and laid her torso on Talyn's chest. She kissed him deeply, her tongue caressing his inside their joined mouths, as Orin shifted her legs behind her so that she knelt over Talyn on all fours. Talyn's hands traveled up her thighs, along her sides, and up to cup her breasts as Orin pushed into her from behind. The thickness of him had her gasping, and she couldn't help but press backward greedily.

"I want you to come for me again," Orin grunted. He reached a hand around to press rhythmically against her clit as his pace quickened. Elaura groaned loudly, breaking from Talyn's lips and pressing her cheek helplessly into his. Orin slammed into her again and again. Heavy breaths tore from his throat, and his skin became slicked with sweat. Elaura's orgasm was swift and stunning, blazing through her in a white hot flash of lightning. It was only seconds more until Orin's dick pulsed hard, and he cried out from his own release.

Legs like jelly, arms shaking, Elaura somehow managed to roll off Talyn and snuggle into his side. Talyn turned to face her even as Orin moved to stretch himself at Talyn's back. Talyn stiffened and Elaura watched as he closed himself off from the intimacy being offered to him. She stroked a hand down his dark cheek, and her eyes softened as she gazed at him. Her beautiful, possessive husband.

"Please stay," she said again.

The echo of her earlier words had him relaxing slightly, and she gently pressed her lips to his. Quietly, Gabriel came to rest behind her, and she turned to him. His arousal pressed against her backside, and she clenched at the thought of him inside of her sensitive flesh. She shifted onto her back, her inner thighs glistening with wetness and desire. Gabriel moved over her, parting her thighs with his, and teased the head of his dick between the folds of her. Despite being filled with the evidence of Orin and Talyn's desire, she suddenly felt empty and wanting. It took nothing to slide inside of her, quick and deep, and he raised her leg to his hip to allow himself even deeper access. Elaura moaned and arched against him, her left hand moving to cup Talyn's cheek. Gabriel leaned forward, pressing his weight onto her. His lips grazed her cheekbone and neck, his teeth scraping the sensitive skin there as he pushed in and out of her, his hips moving in slow waves between her thighs.

She turned her head toward Talyn, her brows drawn together in pleasure as Gabriel's teeth clamped onto her neck. Talyn laid on his side, his hands roaming over her body, and he captured her mouth in his. He cupped her breast, his finger and thumb rolling her nipple back and forth, and she gasped. His hand moved down to rub the center of her as Gabriel moved faster now. Gabriel's breathing was ragged, and he groaned as his hips slapped against Elaura's flesh with every thrust.

Behind Talyn, Orin pushed himself against Talyn's backside. His hands reached around to skim his shoulder, arm, chest, belly. His finger dug into Talyn's hips, and Orin moaned as he pushed his arousal against Talyn. Talyn arched against him, and Orin reached up and soaked a finger in his mouth. He withdrew the wet finger, and slowly drew it down, down, down his body and over the opening of his ass. Orin kissed and nibbled Talyn's back as he slid a finger slowly in and out of him, prepping him for an invasion of a different kind.

Talyn gasped and arched against him, his breathing ragged against Elaura's mouth. She all but screamed as Gabriel lifted her other leg up, pressing both of them into her chest at the knee as he pounded into her. Talyn gasped and tore away from her kiss with a deep growl as Orin pushed his dick into Talyn's ass. He grabbed Talyn's shoulder as Talyn arched into him, taking him as deep as possible. Orin moaned and drove into him again. Talyn sucked in a breath and bit in Elaura's shoulder. His fingers pressed against her clit in rough circles, and

Elaura reached over to stroke the full length of his dick, beads of thick cum appearing at the tip. The urgency in the room was palpable, the bed filled with moaning bodies slicked with sweat and fluids. Their pleasure built and built and built until Elaura cried out just as Orin slammed into Talyn, groaning in something that almost sounded like pain as he came. It was only seconds more until Talyn was emptying himself into Elaura's hand, and Gabriel was exploding inside of her.

The four of them collapsed against one another in a sea of tangled limbs, bodily fluids, and exhausted ecstasy. Their breathing was fast and shallow, their skin slick with glistening sweat. Elaura looked around her and delighted in the way their skin looked against hers. Gabriel's body was atop her, Talyn pressed against her side, and Orin half-draped over Talyn.

Gabriel picked his head up off her chest. His gray eyes, always so sad looking, gazed straight into hers.

"I love you, Elaura," he said.

Before she could answer, he was kissing her and moving inside her again. It wasn't the movements of loving, but more the gentle slide of two people who were not quite ready to let each other go.

Her heart swelled, and she said, "I love you."

She turned to Talyn, who nodded once sternly. Orin kissed Talyn's shoulder, making the man harrumph and frown at him, but he blushed gently despite himself.

"You know I do, too, my little imp," Orin said.

Elaura snuggled deeper into the pile of bodies and closed her eyes.

This.

This was what together was like.

10

It was a strange feeling to be so casually chopping vegetables for dinner as she considered visiting a group of husbands who were not her own. Not that Elaura wanted to at all. Frankly, the thought made her sick to her stomach, but she also dreaded the wrath of the Queens. The conversation with her mother may have made it seem as if the visit was a request, but she knew better.

She should probably tell her husbands—up to now the only things she'd shared with them about the impromptu visit was that her mother had asked how things were getting on and if she'd become pregnant. It wasn't a lie exactly, but it wasn't the whole truth either. If she shared more with her husbands, there was the hope that they could come up with a way to buy her time, but she feared Orin's rash nature and Talyn's possessiveness. Gabriel was the most levelheaded of the group, but he alone wouldn't be able to hold the others back if they decided to remove the men down the hall from the equation or, worse, lash out at the Queen. She couldn't risk either of those things happening.

She glanced at the clock before turning to drop a handful of vegetables into a pan to saute. Her brows drew together. They were late coming home. Nearly an hour by her estimate. There had been another attack the night before, so it was completely plausible the additional patrols and checkpoints simply delayed them. She listened to the sizzle of the vegetables cooking in the hot oil, inhaled the earthy scents of carrots and onion and garlic roasting, and tried not to fear the worst. If she could just focus on the task at hand, time would pass quickly, her men would find their way home, and everything would be as it should be.

As she cooked, her mind wandered to the life she envisioned in the future. She pulled a steaming pork loin from the oven, heat blasting her face when she opened the oven door, and she brushed away the hair that fell across her face. After the revolution, if there ever was one, she imagined many women would leave their pods and find a mate of their choosing. They may even pair off with one man in their pod, one whom they were more closely bonded to. Despite her feelings warming to her current marital situation, she couldn't imagine most women would choose to stay in the arrangement once they had the freedom to leave it. There would inevitably be women who found other women to marry and men who did the same. But what would her pod do?

She was closest to Gabriel, or so it appeared most days, but Orin and Talyn were special to her, too. She loved them all, and her feelings were clearly mutual. It was a strange emotion, one she hadn't planned on. But after the fall, how would she be able to reconcile her involvement in a rebellion with the choice to stay in her arranged marriage? This was, of course, all assuming the Queens' rule even fell during her lifetime. She dreamed about it often enough, but there were no signs it was actually much of a reality. If it did collapse, however, she rather doubted her pod would remain intact. Part of her believed it was only growing because of the pressures they were under—they were all trying to make the best of it. Yet there was a small spark of something else. Hope maybe? Hope that what was blooming inside of her, inside of them, was real. Still, once the pressure of "making due" was gone, there was little doubt in her mind that her marriage would break into tiny pieces, and, she suspected, so would her heart.

With dinner cooked, plated, and going a little cold, Elaura perched anxiously on the edge of a chair and resigned herself to waiting. She twiddled her thumbs, picked at her cuticles, tapped her fingers on the counter to a tune in her head, and was shifting in her seat for the hundredth time when the door opened and they finally stepped inside. Elaura's stomach grumbled loudly even as it lurched in relief, but it turned to concern when they moved into the apartment quickly and pushed the door shut with a jerky shove. Their faces were stony, their breathing rapid. They looked back and forth between each other.

"What happened?" Elaura asked, pushing to her feet and hurrying toward them.

Gabriel looked at her and said, "We had to detour after the meeting. Two scouts were following us."

"Did they know the location?" she asked.

"No, but clearly there's a spy among us," Orin said. He raked a hand through his hair and cursed under his breath.

"You don't know that for sure," Gabriel said, though he didn't sound convinced.

"What will we do now?" Elaura asked.

She rubbed her sweaty palms against the folds of fabric gathered at her waist. She wished for a pair of jeans she'd seen in pictures from the Before or even breeches like the men wore now. Anything that would give her a place to shove her hands. Silly how that was her first thought in this moment.

Orin stalked into the living room and back. He looked like a captive tiger pacing its cage.

"The rebels need to gain access to the Temple Complex. That's the next target. Yesterday's attack was a test, one that didn't go as successfully as we'd hoped," he said.

Elaura moved to stand next to Talyn as he spoke, and she rubbed a hand up and down his back. He grunted and grabbed her hand, pressing a kiss to the inside of her wrist. She gave him a small smile before turning back to Orin.

"Why do they need to get into the Temple?" she asked.

Gabriel hesitated, pulling on his neck for a few minutes. Finally, he answered, "The rebels want to download records of the camps so they can run rescue missions. They hope to build an army of grateful refugees, I suppose. There are also key targets held in those camps, people who could turn the tide of this rebellion once and for all."

"Tell her the rest," Orin demanded.

"Tell me what?" she asked, looking back and forth between Gabriel and Orin.

Gabriel rubbed a hand back and forth across his forehead, pushing aside the short waves of hair that fell there. His brows furrowed, and his eyes crinkled at the corners. He clenched and unclenched his jaw, but still he said nothing. Elaura huffed and crossed her arms.

"Tell me," she said firmly.

Gabriel sucked in a breath. "They want your help to get inside," he said.

"Me? Why me?" Elaura said. She was just the writer, the spinner of propaganda, a shadow lurking behind the actual power of this rebellion. Her greatest asset had always been her proximity to the Queens, the intimate perspective she brought along. What purpose could she serve in some clandestine mission?

"You lived there. You know how to get inside, the movements of the internal staff and the Nurses, the hidden places and passages that no one else knows," Orin said.

"It's out of the question," Gabriel said.

Elaura jerked, as if stunned. "Excuse me?" she said. "I'm fairly sure I can make up my own mind."

"It's too dangerous," Gabriel said, and he folded his arms over his chest as if that was the end of it.

Not that she wanted to be a part of anything, but her pride bristled at being told what she couldn't. "Talyn, you've been quiet. What do you think?" she asked.

"No, I don't want you to go," Talyn said. "I don't want to lose you."

"Orin?" she asked.

Orin shrugged. "I think you should do it. It would be more useful than writing those pamphlets, that's for sure," he said.

"It's too risky, and the majority of us say no," Gabriel said as if that settled it.

"Well, I am part of this, too, and I don't agree. So no, the 'majority' does not. If anything, we're split right down the middle," she argued.

"It's decided," he said firmly.

Elaura blinked in disbelief. His words were a slap in the face to the equitability she'd thought was foundational to their marital success thus far. They were all in this fight to bring freedom to the people of their world, to dethrone a race of alien invaders who'd essentially taken advantage of their moment of need. Among a myriad of rights they hoped to restore was the right to choose your partner or partners, the right to pursue the love you wanted, the life you wanted. Yet here she was, being put firmly in her place by a man as if she should be subservient to him. She'd been subservient to someone her entire life. She would be damned if that would continue now in her marriage.

"It's decided? And you're able to make that decision for me?" she asked.

"We've decided it's what is best for you," Gabriel said.

Orin raised a hand from the nest of his crossed arms and waved, saying, "Uh, not me."

Gabriel ignored him.

"Ah, so this isn't a real marriage at all. You're fighting for freedom for all of them, but not freedom here in our own home," Elaura said, an angry red flush creeping up her cheeks.

"What do you mean, this isn't a 'real marriage?'" Talyn asked in a low voice.

Gabriel's gaze sharpened. "Is it your plan then to work with the rebels, overthrow the Queens, and then choose one of us to ride off into the sunset with?" he asked.

Elaura's flush turned from anger to embarrassment. She had made no such decision, but she couldn't be truthful and say that the possibility hadn't crossed her mind. It shamed her to realize that he'd guessed at her exact thoughts. She opened her mouth to speak, but she didn't know quite what to say. The men looked at her in absolute silence, varying degrees of hurt and anger on Gabriel and Talyn's faces, while Orin's wore a mask of cautious ambivalence. She closed her mouth again, and her arms fell limply against her sides.

"Ah," Gabriel said finally. "So that was your plan, then. Or at least one you considered," he added when she made a small sound of disagreement. "I don't want to risk losing you, but if that's been your thinking this whole time... If you've been sharing words of love while secretly choosing who would ultimately get to keep it... Well, I'd just as soon not find out what you ultimately decide if it comes down to it."

He turned his back on her and, for the very first time, walked into his own room and shut the door.

"I have to go after him," Talyn said, obviously distressed.

Elaura turned to Orin and asked, "What about you?"

Orin leaned back into his hip, his arms still crossed, and shrugged noncommittally.

"This is bigger than anything we might have to sacrifice. Others have lost more," he said.

It wasn't the answer she was hoping for, but it was better than being told what she could and could not do. If that was the best she was going to get, so be it. At no point had she shared her own private thoughts, and never had she said aloud that she would ever give up her husbands should she have the choice. It was unfair to hold those secret fears against her as some sort of precognizant betrayal. Elaura straightened her shoulders, mentally preparing herself for the task ahead, and took a deep breath.

"What do I have to do next?" she asked.

IN THE COMMUNAL BEDROOM, Elaura dressed herself alone. It was rare she was in here alone, without any or all of her husbands to keep her company, and it seemed wrong. The room was too big, noises echoed too loudly, it was too empty. Elaura wrapped herself in a long piece of dark fabric, draping the folds over her body and arranging them to cover her torso. The excess fabric fell around her in waves. She picked up a thick brown belt from her vanity and pulled it tightly around her waist. On the front of the belt, three sets of laces crisscrossed each other in x-shaped patterns. She tied them with fingers that trembled, cursing each time she fumbled with the string.

Elaura tried to convince herself that she was merely nervous or excited even, that her fingers were shaky because she was finally an integral part of a mission—one that would have a more direct impact on the underground revolution than anything she'd ever written. She refused to acknowledge that her hesitation came from the fear that she was losing everything. But she could only lie to herself for so long. By the time she was pulling her hair into a large braid down the center of her head, she'd worked herself into a nice temper to go along with the fear. Her husbands standing against her was only more proof that their marriage was a sham. Even if the Queens were ever deposed and the war ended, she refused to be bound by a marriage that was just as tyrannical.

With one last look in the mirror, Elaura took a

deep breath and walked out of her room with a swish of skirts. Gabriel was no longer in his bedroom, and he and Talyn sat together on the couch. Their bodies were separate except for Gabriel's hand on Talyn's thigh. Their posture was stiff, and neither met her gaze as they stared at the program flashing across the screen before them. It was a live broadcast of the Sunday Mass, a weekly spiritual ceremony that was as much propaganda as it was inspiration. Of course, there was a delay on the live feed—the Queens couldn't allow for a real-time broadcast, especially with the rebel attacks on the rise. Delays aside, the Mass was an ideal time for Elaura to blend into the crowds and infiltrate the Temple. While the Queens spoke their wisdom, warned of a second coming of the plague should the people ignore their words, and screamed about penance and vigilance, people and soldiers alike would be distracted.

Orin walked out of the hallway and crossed the living room. "Are you ready?" he asked.

Elaura nodded and followed him to the front door. She glanced back at Gabriel and Talyn. Talyn stared resolutely ahead, refusing to look at her, but Gabriel's eyes were sad and pleading. She could hear his voice in her head. *You don't have to do this.*

But she did. She was tired of living like this, tired of seeing women beaten or dying, their deaths covered up and dismissed by a fertility obsessed tyrant. Elaura finally had the chance to do more than put words on a piece of paper, to take action. She was finally going to be of some actual use, and she wasn't about to let them take that away from her.

She squared her shoulders and swept out of the apartment.

11

Elaura's skirts spun around her ankles and slapped against Orin's legs as she moved to stand next to him. He reached for the door and hesitated. He turned to her, and it crossed his mind that she looked like some warrior princess heading off to battle. She'd braided her hair away from her face and set her shoulders firm. She looked determined and strong, as if she had finally stepped into her power.

"Are we going?" Elaura asked.

Orin raised his eyes to hers and shook his head. "You're going," he said.

"Alone?" she asked, brows drawn together.

He nodded.

"I don't understand."

"It's best if you go alone. To avoid any extra attention."

He considered the mission they were about to embark on. It would be risky. He didn't think his little wife, innocent warrior that she was, truly grasped the torture that awaited them if they were captured. There were unknown ways in which it could go terribly wrong, but despite the danger (or rather, because of it), his blood heated. He reached for her and yanked her to him, spinning their bodies until the wall was firmly against her back. He pressed his body to hers, grinding his hips into her.

"What are you doing?" she asked in surprise.

"I'm not good with words," he said. It was the truth. Their mission loomed before them, bringing with it a flurry of emotions he struggled to give voice to. All he could do was show her. He had to. She had to know exactly why she had to come home safe to them all. It was the only option.

With a curse, Orin crushed his mouth down on hers, smothering her gasp. He didn't care that they were in full view of Gabriel and Talyn. All he cared about was her wrapped around him, of being inside her right now. He yanked up her skirts, letting them bunch around her waist and over his arms as he hiked up her leg. It didn't matter that it would be fast and rough. In fact, needed it like that. He needed her now. His fingers deftly undid the laces on his breeches, and, with a shift of his hips, he drove inside her with one powerful thrust. She gasped, her flesh smarting at the intrusion, but the pain was mixed with pleasure, and she arched against him. Her arms gripping his shoulders with white knuckles, and he growled as he pounded into her. It was everything he could do not to explode immediately.

Finally, she cried out, and he felt her muscles clench rhythmically around him. She shuddered as the orgasm rippled through her body, bringing him to the peak of his own pleasure. He growled again, the sound low and primal against her neck, and spilled himself into her. They throbbed together for a moment, their foreheads pressed together. Elaura looked up at him with a sheepish smile. He wanted to kiss her. He wanted to soothe her and tell her this mission would succeed, but a fear consumed him as powerful as his desperation for her had been. With a cry, he tore himself from her, her skirts dropping to the floor with a rustling sound, and stalked past a now empty couch to his room.

A door slammed down the hall, and Elaura stood alone in a home that might as well have been empty for all the comfort it held.

~

ELAURA WAS STILL stunned when she walked the streets below their apartment building. Orin had seemed the least affected by her decision to take on this mission. That is until he'd taken against the wall like a wild beast in front of the other husbands and then slammed off into his room. Her skin was still hot where he'd touched her, but she wasn't sure if her cheeks were flushed from arousal or anger. With a deep breath, she forced herself to focus on the task at hand. It wouldn't do to walk into Mass with fiery hot cheeks and a daydreamer's expression. Any loss of focus right now could be catastrophic to not only the mission, but to her own safety.

Following the instructions from Orin, she slipped down a narrow alley. She looked both ways before ducking into it to make sure she wasn't being watched. At the end of the alley, there was a doorway. Inside it, she'd find her Shadow, essentially a handler who managed information and kept tabs on her whereabouts. Or rather, she wouldn't find them at all, but they would be there all the same. Aptly named, her Shadow would be a silent presence haunting her steps, ready to report her successes—and failures—to the rebel leaders.

"Security room immediately after the service," a voice whispered as she passed.

Elaura's steps slowed, and she angled her head slightly toward the voice. "And the disk?" she asked, her words but a whisper.

"Nurse Kier will find you," the voice said.

Elaura's brows furrowed. It was rare to have someone working on the inside, rarer still for that person to be a Nurse. She resisted the urge to ask more and continued down the alley. From the distant town square, the bells rung to mark the top of the hour. Nine tolls in all. Hurrying now, Elaura exited the alley through the back, looping around until she returned to the main street. Mass would begin soon, and she needed to make sure there was nothing about her arrival that stood out.

As she neared the Temple, the crowds on the streets grew denser. The Queens didn't require attending Mass, but there was a widespread belief (and rumors supported it) that people who didn't attend were carefully cataloged and monitored. The wide red doors to the Temple stood open in welcome, a Nurse stationed at either side. Soldiers milled through the crowd both outside and in, though they held no weapons today. As totalitarian as the Queens' rule was, they must appear to be gentle and protective. Knowing their power and stature so intimately, Elaura shuddered to think what it would be like to see them as anything else.

She swept into the main worship room, disguised within the crowd. She knew there was a shift change between security and the Nurses immediately following Mass, and it would be her best chance of getting into the security room.

She took a seat in a pew near the back of the room. This part of the building was originally a church from the Before, so the benches all faced an altar on the far side of the room and curved around it in rows. There was a podium placed in the center of the altar, and there were three regal chairs equally spaced behind it. Music from a harp served as background noise to the procession of the Queens. They walked into the room from behind the wall at the back of the altar, dressed in flowing togas of pure white with golden lace embroidered along the hems and magnificent crowns atop their heads. Two took their seats on the golden chairs, and one moved to stand at the podium.

"Welcome," the Queen said. "Before we begin today, I want us all to look around at one another. Look to your left and your right, to your brothers and your sisters. Think about what they mean to you, what this community means to you. We all work in it together. We feed one another. We comfort each other. And yet there are those who would seek to tear us apart, to take our brothers and sisters, husband and wives, our very children from us. The plague came because this world was dark and evil and sick. It made you sicker. It took your babies, sometimes even your very lives. But we have overcome! Together, we have pulled ourselves out of the darkness. We have reformed our society, rebuilt our cities, and now we welcome new life into our communities."

Elaura watched as the Queens rose from their chairs and raised their arms in tandem. Their robes fell to the floor in ripples of fabric over their arms, and it seemed to shift like liquid. The light from above cast a glow over the altar, creating a god-like appearance on their already alien faces.

A Nurse guided a woman, her belly heavy with child, up to the altar. She stood next to the Queen, her eyes wide in adoration. Other women around the room stood and made their way toward the front.

"We must remain vigilant to protect this life," the Queen said, her hands pressed to the woman's round belly. The harp music began again, and the procession of pregnant women began, each walking up to receive their blessing. The Queen bent low to press her hands on each woman's belly.

The rest of the Mass passed in a blur of fear mongering and hollow inspirational words that vaguely echoed those from the past. Once, when Elaura was young, her friend had secreted a banned book about religion, one of the few surviving copies, into their rooms. The descriptions of the beliefs and practices of ancient humans throughout the world had fascinated her. It seemed like much of humanity at the time was spiritual, at least in some sense of the word. Ironically, she thought, that was probably why the Queens' rule was so effective. They ritualized every aspect of life, as if by doing so they gave it all some deeper meaning. In actuality, it was about control. Control and fear.

When it was finally over, Elaura stood and

followed the crowd into the narthex, a sort of lobby that stood between the altar room and the outside. Here the Nurses would engage in conversation with the attendees, and it was also one of the few times when everyday people could have direct contact with the Queens. They meandered through the periphery of the crowd, stooping slightly in mock humility to avoid towering over the people. Elaura marked the Queens' movements, ensuring she remained undetected. Her mother was not among them today, so she was less likely to be noticed, a small blessing to be sure.

"Psst..." a voice whispered behind her.

Elaura turned to see a Nurse smiling at her stiffly.

In a more moderate voice, the woman said, "Blessings upon you, child. How goes your marriage?"

"Nurse Kier?" Elaura mouthed silently. The woman inclined her head with a meaningful look in her eye and held out her hands. Elaura took the hint and grasped them with a smile, embracing her as if they were old friends. "I'm a happy wife indeed. May children bless us soon."

Nurse Kier slid her hands away, leaving a small disk resting in one palm of Elaura's hand and a square chip in the other. She closed her fist over it and pulled her hands into her robes.

"We can only hope. Many blessings to you all,"

Nurse Kier said, and then she continued her procession around the room.

As casually as possible, Elaura threaded through the crowd toward the side of the narthex. Her pulse was racing, her blood roared in her ears, and her movements felt stiff and unnatural, but she forced her feet to keep a steady pace. Finally, she reached the door and moved from the narthex into a long hallway typically used by the Queens and Nurses, along with the various staff and family members who attended the Queens. It made a near complete circle throughout the entire Complex and was the fastest way to navigate all the buildings. As Elaura hoped, it was filled with others hurrying along with their work.

Elaura hastened through the corridor, arranging her face so that she seemed engrossed in whatever task she'd been assigned. She smiled at people who passed her, even recognizing some from the life living in the Temple, and that they smiled back made her feel confident in her ruse. As she moved, she wondered how many times she'd run down these halls as a child, her tiny bare feet slapping against the stones beneath them. She missed the innocence of such a time, when the true nature of the world hid and everything seemed perfect and magical. When she approached the security room, Elaura held her breath and slowed her gait. Outside the room was a golden box with a small slit in it that glowed red. The square disk hidden in her hand would get her through the first door with ease, but there was only one thing that would gain her entry into the protected chamber within...

The voice of a Queen.

12

Elaura estimated the previous shift of personnel would leave for Mass any minute now, so she stopped a few feet from the door and pretended to adjust her shoe. The seconds stretched into minutes like a piece of taffy being drawn into endless lengths, and she could hear her breath despite the noise of the corridor. People hurried past her, a wash of colors and fabrics and smells, but she barely noticed them. Finally, when she thought she could procrastinate no more, the door to the security room opened and two men stepped out. They had dark skin and hair clipped short in the same style as the soldiers.

The men pulled the door shut behind them, and Elaura heard the click of the automatic lock. The sound was familiar to Elaura, instantly pulling her back to her youth when she and a few of the other girls had sneaked into the security room to watch the Queens and their private rituals on the cameras inside. Except for the bedrooms and showers, the cameras monitored every room in the complex. Elaura figured she had scant minutes before the next shift arrived, possibly less. She slid the square chip into the glowing slot on the wall panel, holding her breath while it scanned. When the lock clicked, Elaura released the breath in a rush. She turned the handle of the door and quickly slipped inside.

Countless screens lined the wall to her left in rows. A control panel below them allowed for an innumerable number of actions to be taken, sounding alarms being one of them. To the right, there was another door that was Elaura's true target. She was not here for information about the Temple Complex. No, she was here for information far more valuable than that.

She stashed the square chip in a hidden pocket sewn into the inside of her belt and walked to the inner door. Unlike the plain door behind her, this one had a swirling pattern inlaid in its metal, and in the very center, there was a sculpture of a vulva. Its opening spread wide, the clitoris jutting out proudly, doubling as both an anatomic element and a microphone. It represented femininity and pleasure and the power of a woman's body, the gateway to her womb in the same way that this door was another kind of gateway.

Stepping up to the sculpture, Elaura took a deep breath. Her skin was hot and tingling, her pulse racing. It was said that only a Queen could unlock the door with their alien trill, a sound so foreign to human ears and yet hauntingly beautiful. A human's vocal chords could not imitate the sound, but the Queens had forbidden their daughters from even attempting it, half-breeds that they were. The secrets such a noise could unlock must be dear indeed for such a law, and the punishment for disobeying was severe—the complete removal of the voice box. To her knowledge, no daughter had ever dared for fear of it.

Elaura glanced quickly behind her, ensuring she was still safe and alone. She took a deep breath and filled her lungs to bursting. She positioned the tip of her tongue on the roof of her mouth, opened her throat, pursed her lips, and pitched her voice high. At first the sound was off key, and her voice broke. Sweat beaded up on Elaura's skin and her stomach turned to knots. She tried again, and again she failed to form the sound that would open the lock. Hundreds of nameless people were counting on her, people imprisoned in camps for bucking against their subjugation, people who remembered a better time, however flawed it may have been. How many had died fighting for it? How many more would die if she didn't succeed?

At that moment, the weight of the world seemed

to rest on her shoulders, and she had to hurry. The next set of guards would be here soon. Almost desperately, she raised her chin, repositioned her tongue, and drew in one final breath. Opening her throat, she pushed her jaw forward and held her tongue to the tip of her teeth, the top of it pressed flat against the roof of her mouth. She exhaled a powerful breath, and the sound that emerged was musical. Though wobbly at first, the note grew in power and intensity, and pride welled in Elaura's chest.

When at last she ended the note, she heard the crisp click of the lock, and the door jerked inward ever so slightly. Elaura breathed a sigh of relief and pushed it open, stepping inside the room. She wasted no time and scanned the room for the backup port that would allow her to download the security system's information. On a desk to the left, she found it and pushed the clear disk into the slot. She didn't know what would happen next and could only hope everything from here would be automatic. When the red light next to the port began blinking, Elaura assumed the download had begun, and she waited.

Suddenly, from outside the room, there were voices. Her ears pricked when she heard them, and her pulse quickened as she stared at the port, willing the download to finish. With an almost inaudible click, the light turned from red to green, and she ejected the small disk. Elaura tucked it into the hidden pocket of her belt along with the chip before bolting out of the rooms as fast as her feet would carry her. She carefully closed the door to the main security room and moved several feet down the corridor before stopping to catch her breath. She pressed her back to the wall, holding a hand to her chest as if that would stop her heart from beating against it.

Overhead, the bell tolled the hour. It was ten o'clock in the morning, and soon they would release a second service of worshipers into the narthex. Elaura looked quickly left and right and hurried back down the corridor. She made her way into the narthex and did her best to blend in with the people just beginning to mill about. Soon, she would pass the disks to her Shadow who would deliver them to those who could decrypt the data and use it.

On the far side of the room, she spotted her Shadow and slowly began making her way over to her. She discreetly pulled the chip and disk from her belt, palming them and hiding her hand in the folds of her skirt. Passing her Shadow, they brushed hands as if touching by pure coincidence as they passed, and she transferred her previous cargo. Before she'd taken a few steps more, her Shadow had already disappeared, and she was free to make her way out of the complex as quickly as possible.

Stepping out into the courtyard, she hugged her

arms tight against the cold. Funny how it hadn't bothered her this much before. She bundled her hands in her skirts to keep them warm and hurried around the perimeter of the courtyard toward home, but as she reached the cobblestone walkway, two figures emerged from behind the towering pillars on either side. Without a word, they loomed over her, one on each side, and grabbed her by the arms.

"What are you doing?" she said, trying in vain to pull her arms from their grip. Their fingers dug into the tender skin at her elbow, and she cried out in pain when they only tightened their grip against her struggles.

She opened her mouth to scream. A cloth came over her face from someone behind her, and she breathed in a sickly sweet smell before she realized what was happening. She became lightheaded and weak. Then the world went black, and she slumped to the ground between her captors.

TALYN KNEW his pacing was driving Orin and Gabriel mad, but he couldn't help it. He had to move, to do something, anything except sit and wait for Elaura to return. Her words had cut deeply, but he'd also seen her eyes when they'd made love. He was with her when she'd finally let down her walls and embraced them all together. It was in that moment that his has come down, too. They had become an actual family, even if she wasn't ready to accept it.

"Can't you sit down, Talyn?" Orin groaned.

Talyn ignored him.

"You're going to walk through the floor if you keep that up," Orin said.

He sat on the couch with his legs spread wide, slouching into the cushions behind him. His long hair fell in waves over the side of his face, and he wore an expression that told the world he couldn't care less about what was happening at the moment, but the heel of his foot tapped up and down in time with Talyn's footsteps and gave him away.

"Leave him alone, Orin," Gabriel said with a sigh.

"I just don't see—" Orin broke off as his phone buzzed on the counter across the room.

He jumped up and sprinted to it, answering before the second ring. Gabriel and Talyn watched him as he listened to the voice on the other side, his responses curt and predominantly one or two words. Talyn watched Orin's expression change from confusion to rage, his jaw flexing rhythmically as he listened.

"Is there no plan for—" Orin said, stopping again at the voice on the other end spoke. His eyes darkened suddenly, and he roared, "Fuck you all!" He slammed the phone on the counter, shattering it into shards of glass and metal. He looked at Talyn and Gabriel, his chest heaving. "Elaura's been taken."

"What? How? When?" Gabriel asked, already on his feet. His voice filled with worry, but his eyes betrayed a mind already working to solve the problem.

"We told her not to go!" Talyn exploded. Just now, he couldn't tell if he was directing his rage more at Elaura or her captors. All he knew was if she had listened to them, she would still be here.

"Don't say it like it's her fault," Orin said.

"They aren't planning an extraction?" Gabriel asked, but it was not really a question.

No rescue. Talyn knew what that meant. They all did. Elaura was a daughter of a Queen. Her torture would be extensive, the punishment if she survived would be death, and not the kind that was kind or quick. They would make an example of her, hang her body along the city walls as a message.

"Why would they abandon her? Did she fail somehow?" Gabriel asked, his brows drawn together. It made little sense to him why they would throw aside such a valuable asset to the rebellion.

Orin shook his head. "Worse. She succeeded. Her Shadow retrieved the information. Everything about the prisoners, supply lines, everything—and it's all far more valuable than her. In their minds, her part in this rebellion is over in, and her sacrifice was a noble one," he said mockingly. "They said it like she's already dead."

"Is she?" Talyn demanded. The knot in his stomach tightened.

"I don't think so. Pilots are on their way to attack the camps now. The war starts tonight. Why waste the resources on her? They don't need her anymore."

"We do. We have to get her," Talyn said, his hands fisted at his sides.

"We won't last five minutes running into a fully staffed prison to try," Orin said. "Besides, she said it herself. This marriage is a sham. Why should we risk our necks when her intention was to leave us all along?"

"You don't mean that," Gabriel said. "We saw you with her. You love her, just as we do."

"Nice speech, but no. I saw the betrayal on your face. You feel exactly the same as I do," Orin said. "And I'm not in the mood to die over her."

"Not in the mood?" Talyn said. He stalked over to where Orin stood and poked a finger in his chest. "You know what they're doing to her every second we leave her with them!"

"Yes, and I don't want them to do it to me, so kindly get your fucking hand off me," Orin said, his eyes flashing dangerously.

Talyn believed there was a time for peace and a time for violence, and right then, he chose violence.

Without another word, he slammed his fist into Orin's jaw with a sickening crack.

"Talyn!" Gabriel yelled. He made a move to go to Orin, but the pretty boy waved him away, his hand on his cheek. Orin pulled his fingers away from the side of his mouth, blood coating the tips of them.

"I deserved that, but I'm still not going. If you two want to die trying to save a woman who doesn't want you, be my guest. Me? I'll save myself the drama," Orin said, and he stalked past them both and slammed the door to his room.

"We have to get her, Gabriel. We can't leave her like that. I don't care what she said or what she'll do. We can't leave her," Talyn said, his voice becoming more desperate with every word.

Gabriel nodded. "How's your hand?" he asked.

"Hurts like the devil."

"You know, I've never really believed in one," Gabriel said thoughtfully. "A devil, that is."

"We may well find out tonight."

"Yes, we may."

13

Gabriel tried to stay calm as he and Talyn prepared to infiltrate the prison with no backup. Because they were part of the rebellion, they were lucky to have at least bare minimum protection and some weapons. However, bullet-proof vests would do nothing to protect their heads or limbs. Not to mention they couldn't very well walk down the street casually sporting even the most minimal armor and weapons. The soldiers would kill them in a second. They had to be smart, clever. So they concealed knives in their boots, rough lengths of cord in their pockets, and small guns in holsters under their shirts. They wore their vests over a thin undershirt and draped a looser fitting shirt over it.

Gabriel and Talyn left the apartment once they'd armed and protected themselves as best they could.

Gabriel considered going to Orin's door to convince him to join them. At the very least, they could use his help. In the end, though, he decided against it. A man had the right to choose his own fate, but the consequences would be his to bear.

Consequences.

Now that was a word that filled him with shame. He'd virtually thrown her to the wolves with his stupidity. Just like the Queens, he'd tried to bring down an exacting power upon her. He'd hoped to help her avoid danger, but his words had only strengthened her desire to put herself in such a dangerous position. If they made it out of this alive, he'd spend the next lifetime making it up to her. He'd ensure she would never again have to choose between her beliefs and her family. Their marriage was not a sham. Maybe it was a seedling, a plant in its infancy, but it was true and loving. When he brought her home, he'd make sure she knew that every second of every day until forever.

Talyn knew the streets and alleys better than Gabriel, so Gabriel fell in step behind him as they slid through the shadows. Night had descended by then and a curfew was in place, giving them all the more reason to stay in the shadows to avoid detection. As they rounded a corner, Talyn raised a hand and had them pressing against the wall. Gabriel waited. Footsteps echoed behind them, and even the blood roaring in his ears couldn't cover the sound.

They waited in the dark as the steps grew closer and closer. His breath turned to smoke in the ice cold air, and he slowed his breathing lest the wisps of it give them away. The footsteps slowed as they reached their hiding place, and his muscles bunched in anticipation.

"Good. I've found you," a voice whispered.

It was Orin. Gabriel briefly glimpsed his face before he slid into the shadows beside them. Talyn muffled a curse.

"You came," Gabriel said.

"So, I did," Orin said with a shrug.

"See? You do love her."

"Shut up."

"Quiet, both of you," Talyn whispered forcefully. "Let's go."

He started walking and Gabriel followed close behind, Orin at his back. Despite knowing they'd likely die tonight, Gabriel was confident they'd at least successfully rescue their wife. They'd be dead by morning almost certainly, but he still thought their chances were at least a little better now. They wound their way through a maze of streets and passageways, even going through a few abandoned buildings, and Gabriel was sure they doubled back on their own trail several times. The moon was high above them and Gabriel's lunges burned from exertion in the frozen air when they finally reached the prison. Unlike the reinforced camps outside the city, surrounded by barbed wire and military machinery, the Hall of Inquisition was a subtler prison. Here, authorities detained individuals like political activists, interrogated, and most often executed them, and by "interrogated," they meant tortured until they had no more information to give up. The worst of it happened in the camps outside the city walls, but it was more likely Elaura wasn't there yet, even if that was her eventual destination.

The three men waited, watched, and listened. Before they could attempt entry, they needed to figure out how many men were inside, where Elaura was being kept, and how to get her out. They were flying blind, and the thought filled Gabriel with rage. How dare their leaders put Elaura in danger and then leave her to rot once she'd served her purpose? It was eerily similar to their current government, and for the first time, Gabriel doubted if the rebellion would truly repair the world.

He looked up to the moon, offering a silent prayer to whatever almighty thing might exist up there. Even if all he could do was buy her time to escape, it would be worth it. As he watched the stars twinkling around the glowing moon, the sky began to move. Only it wasn't the sky moving, he realized, it was hovercrafts flying over. They filled the sky, hundreds of them. Before he could get the attention of Orin or Talyn, the sirens wailed all around them, and then the world exploded.

Bombs whistled as they fell from the sky and crashed into the city. It was clear the Temple was the primary target, though more landed on the monuments scattered close by, spraying bits of rock and debris over them as they exploded. The air filled with dust and acrid smoke. His ears rung, and his lungs burned with every breath he took. Gabriel watched as soldiers ran in groups around them, and he heard the sharp bangs of gunfire only blocks away. Here, the curfew might prove to be a godsend, saving the civilians already home for the night.

Suddenly, soldiers came running from a stairway that descended into the underbelly of the city, the entrance to the prison. Talyn shoved them all back against the wall. They waited for the sound of heavy boots to fade, then Talyn signaled for them to follow him below. Gabriel moved close behind. They needed to hurry. The attacks would be a distraction for the remaining guards, and this was their best chance.

Talyn opened the door at the bottom of the stairs, and they filed in, their feet shuffling on the concrete floor. Above their heads, the yellow emergency lights had turned on, and the roof shook with every bomb that dropped onto the city above. Concrete dust showered on them from cracks that streaked ominously across the ceiling. Gabriel walked half-sideways, foot over foot, along the wall as they crept slowly down the hallway. They passed countless empty desks and offices, computers left open, papers scattered across the floor. It was clear the staff had already left in a hurry and not out the main entrance, likely when the power went out. They came to a closed door with bars reinforcing the glass. Gabriel tried to pull it open, but it didn't so much as budge.

"Is this where they keep them?" Gabriel asked.

Talyn nodded, and they began searching for a button or switch of some kind that would open it. When the door suddenly swung open with a loud beep, Gabriel turned around to see Orin removing his hand from a switch on the desk behind them. Orin shrugged, and Gabriel nodded in appreciation. They proceeded to the cells beyond. As they walked, the smell of blood and sweat and urine assaulted his nose. He glanced into the cells they passed and saw prisoners in various states of dress and injury, all shot point blank in the head. His stomach sank as he realized the guards had systematically executed the captives, likely at the very start of the attack.

With a fisted hand held high, Talyn motioned for them to stop, and Gabriel heard voices talking up ahead. He slowly drew the largest knife from his boot and watched as Orin and Talyn did the same. They knew they had a better chance of getting Elaura out alive if they were as quiet as possible. Even as he thought about it, he reached into his shirt to click the safety off his gun. If it came down to it, he might need to draw it quickly. As they came to the end of the hallway, he and Talyn positioned themselves at either corner. Gabriel peeked around it and saw her.

Elaura sagged against wrist restraints that held her strapped to an x-shaped contraption. Blood stained her toga, and it fell about her in ripped folds. They'd left her belt on, and its brown leather had gone black with blood. Wisps of hair had slipped out of her braid, falling around a face that was bloody and bruised. She didn't appear conscious, but she still breathed.

Three men stood around her dressed in military uniforms with badges that indicated their high rank. One stood off to the side of Elaura, his hands holding a rifle across the front of his body, and another sat at a compact desk, listening to whatever communication was coming through the device in his ear. His fingers working over a transparent computer pad laid flat in front of him. The last man of the group was clearly the more active participant in Elaura's torture. His uniform was speckled with bits of her blood, and he held a baton that had two metal prongs on one end. Standing close to Elaura, the man lifted her chin with a finger and spoke in her ear. She opened her eyes and lifted her eyes to his, glaring at him mutinously, but she didn't respond. He stared at her for a moment, then without warning, he pressed the metal prongs against her body. She screamed, and her entire body convulsed.

Gabriel watched Talyn's fists clench at his sides, all the muscles in his arms bunching, and then he was running around the corner. Wordlessly, Orin and Gabriel followed, spreading out to handle the other men in the room as Talyn wrestled the man with the baton. Gabriel stepped behind the seated man, gripping the back of his head and slamming his face into the desk. He grasped a handful of the stunned man's hair, yanked his head back, and swiftly drew the knife across his throat, sneering as the blood spurted across the computer panel.

Across from him, Orin grabbed the soldier's rifle with one hand and plunged the short knife he carried down into the man's neck. A shot rang out in the confined space, and the man crumpled to the ground in a puddle of blood. Gabriel turned to see Talyn kneeling on the man with the baton, his fists slamming into his face again and again, knuckles split and bleeding. His ears rang, his vision blurred, and the room slanted. Orin's movements caught his attention, and his lips moved, but he couldn't hear anything but the ringing. Pain exploded across his body, and he looked down to see blood pouring down his chest. His eyes were wide when he met Orin's gaze again. Then the world went black, and he sank to his knees.

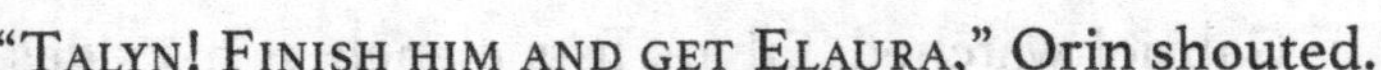

"TALYN! FINISH HIM AND GET ELAURA," Orin shouted.

Talyn, his chest heaving and his entire torso covered with splatters of his and the soldier's blood, stopped pummeling the man long enough to look around the room. The sight of Gabriel on the ground snapped him out of his rage, and in a split second, he drew his knife out of his waistband and across the man's neck, leaving behind a deep gash that barely bled. Orin rushed to Gabriel, tearing lengths of cloth from the dead man's uniform and stuffing it into the hole in his chest. It was high and to Gabriel's right, and Orin prayed it had missed any organs or arteries. Tears pricked at his eyes as he saw how much blood Gabriel was losing, and he knew they were on borrowed time.

"You can't die. You hear me," he said, his voice breaking.

With his hand pressed hard against the cloths already soaked with blood, he blinked the tears away and hefted Gabriel's left arm over his shoulders to anchor him. He lifted his limp form upright and looked over to see Talyn finally free Elaura from her restraints. She leaned against him, and while she was clearly weak, she was standing, and he was proud of his mighty little warrior.

"We've got to get out of here," Orin said.

His heart seemed to beat in time with the gunfire

outside, his skin slicked with sweat. Since joining the rebels, he'd prepared for the day when he would be called to war, but he'd never imagined it would be like this.

They made their way out the same way they'd come in, grateful that no one else appeared to stop them. As they ascended the stairs outside, Orin heard the bells tolling. Odd, he thought to himself. The bells never made a sound in the evening hours. Elaura reached out a hand and grabbed his arm. He looked down at where her fingers curled around him and then at her, his eyes filling with regret. Because of his anger and pride, he'd almost left her to die, and he promised himself that never again would he leave her side. Her tongue darted out to lick her lips, and she spoke in a hoarse voice.

"I have to find my mother."

14

Whether by nature or willpower, Elaura felt her strength returning. She took a deep breath and stood as straight as she could manage. She had at least one broken rib on the left side, with many more bruised. The places where the metal prod had touched her skin burned, but even that was fading. Blood covered her still, but there was nothing to be done about it for now.

"I have to find my mother," she said to Orin, her hand clutching his arm tightly.

He looked down at it and then back at her. His eyes were so sad, and she wondered why, but he simply nodded. No questioning her, no arguments. Simple agreement. After everything that had led to this, it was admittedly refreshing to be listened to without question.

Orin dragged Gabriel up the stairs, Talyn

helping to bear some of the weight, and Elaura followed. They departed the prison the same way she'd been brought into it, albeit with less chaos than was currently happening around them. After more than an hour with sirens and bombs dropping overhead, it was eerie to hear relative quiet when they emerged. Random spurts of gunfire still echoed in the background, and nothing could drown out the cries of the dead and dying, but it was silent compared to the barrage of sound before.

They moved around rubble and bodies until they reached the courtyard and the entrance to the Temple. It was heavily in ruin, and the remnants of soldiers lay everywhere. There were relatively few dressed in civilian clothes, which both common people and the rebels wore, and Elaura estimated the Queens' forces had taken heavy losses, at least on the ground. She picked her way through the debris and tried to keep her breathing even and shallow. It hurt less like that.

"Through there," she said, pointing to a partially collapsed archway that eventually led to the private chambers of the Queens and their children.

This was the place where she'd grown up. Looking around brought on a barrage of complicated emotions. This was her home for so long, somewhere she'd romped and laughed and learned so much... and yet, it was a place of tyranny, a palace devoted to subjugation and lies.

They traveled down endless halls, and no matter which side of the conflict they were on, the people who ran past them or huddled in corners paid them no mind. When they reached her mother's chamber, Elaura signaled she would go in alone, so Orin gently propped Gabriel against the wall. Elaura turned to him and raised a hand to his cheek.

"Stay here. Help him," she said, and laid a gentle kiss on his lips. "I love you."

He grabbed her hand and held it to his cheek, turning his face into it to press a kiss to her palm. "I love you," he said hoarsely.

Elaura turned to Talyn next and said, "Three doors down, there is a door that leads to a short hallway. In the closet at the end, you'll find at least one emergency medical kit. It should have enough in it to keep Gabriel alive."

His hands came to her face, and his brows drew together as his dark eyes searched hers.

"We are a family. You are ours, and we are yours."

Tears formed in the corners of Elaura's eyes and slipped down her cheeks, and she nodded. His mouth came down on hers for but a moment before he was tearing himself away and running down the hall. She watched him go for a moment. Then she kneeled down in front of Gabriel, cupping his face in her hands. The tears were pouring out now, and her throat was hot and tight.

"Gabriel, I don't know if you can hear me, but

you have to pull through this. You have to. I don't care what deals you have to make with the gods. You live, damn you. You live!" she said.

Pressing her face against his, she closed her eyes and sobs wracked her body. She prayed to every deity she'd ever read about, made promises to the devil, and begged the universe that her husbands came out of this whole. When Gabriel shifted beneath her, she drew back and watched his eyelashes flutter open. With a cry, she pressed her lips to his.

"I love you," he said, his voice barely a whisper.

"I love you," she said.

She pressed another kiss to his lips and stood, squeezing Orin's hand one more time before she pushed open the door to her mother's chamber. She stifled a shudder when it slammed ominously behind her.

She made her way to her mother's receiving room, thinking of the type of woman her mother was and assuming that would be where she'd make her last stand. She was right. Despite nothing having technically changed since her last visit, there was a distinct aura of decadence that was missing. No servants or Nurses bustled around to attend, no glittering decanter of wine stood on the table beside her, and no fire roared in the grate. Her mother simply laid, as regal as ever, on the chaise, her body stretched out as if the world around wasn't crumbling after all.

"Why are you still here?" Elaura asked, stopping to stand by an ornate side table lined with tiny drawers filled with treasures and candles and perfumes.

Her mother looked at her, her angled eyes seeming almost bored by her presence, but not surprised.

"What is that expression humans have? A captain goes down with his ship," the Queen said, her hand waving dismissively in the air. "Oh, Elaura, I wish you could've seen our home planet. You may not have appreciated it fully, half-breed that you are, but it was beautiful. Trees as tall as mountains, three suns that danced together across the sky, and rivers and lakes like liquid sapphire."

"If it was so beautiful, why come here?" Elaura asked.

Her mother shrugged, the gesture a sequence of elegant movements that flowed into one another like flowing water. "A plague decimated our home. Ironic, I know. It wiped out nearly all life, animals and plants alike. Those of us who were left quickly discovered ourselves barren. We knew we would never recover, and so we set out among the stars. Each time we thought we'd found sanctuary proved to be a false hope. Until we found Earth," her mother said.

"Why come here if the humans were suffering from the same disease? Why breed with them if you'd only watch your people, your children, die again?" Elaura asked.

This was why she was here. This was why she'd sought her mother. In these last moments, she needed to know.

"We brought it with us, of course," the Queen said, and there was a callousness about her tone.

Elaura's jaw dropped, and the air rushed out of her lungs.

"What?"

"Of course, we watched Earth for quite some time before we made it our home. We saw how easily humans were to control, how desperate they were for answers, so desperate, in fact, that they warred with one another constantly. We altered the plague and released it upon the humans. Yes, we killed many and made others sterile, but it was for the greater good. Truly, it was no greater casualty than what they inflicted upon themselves," said the Queen. She took a deep breath, as if to talking about the murder and subjugation of billions was exhausting. "We'd been so long without a home, you see, so alone in the universe. But with one little decision, we would be gods again."

"Why are you telling me this?" Elaura asked.

Her mother shrugged. "It amuses me."

Elaura's face was a mask of rage and disgust. She

stared at her mother mutinously. "All those people. You did all of this? Murdered millions in order to what... be worshiped? You cared nothing for them, or for me."

All the years of her life, she'd struggled with feeling inadequate, feeling unloved. It was why she'd initially sought anything she could find about the Before. She'd had to know if all children felt this way.

"Care for you? You were nothing. A half-breed created to flatter the humans. Pawns in a game you'll never understand no matter how much of my blood runs through your veins," the Queen said. She sighed, her long gown rustling over her body, and she turned her face away from Elaura as if to dismiss her.

Elaura's hands fisted at her sides, her skin pressing against the fabric caked in dried blood, and then something cold and hard was against her fist. She looked down and saw Orin, crouched behind the table, slipping a long dagger into her fingers. Her eyes widened, and he nodded once. She buried her hand in the folds of her dress and walked toward her mother. Her face was emotionless, her steps slow and measured.

"What are you about, child?" her mother asked.

"I'm no longer a child, mother. I'm a Queen," Elaura said.

In a single motion, she slashed her mother's

throat with the knife, the sharp blade slicing deep into her neck. Blood poured from the wound in a waterfall down her body. The red liquid soaked through her mother's gown and spread down the fabric. Surprise lit her eyes, and she clawed at her neck in vain. Then the river of blood slowed, her frantic movements stopped, and her eyes closed. Her long, elegant body slumped into the chair, her head dropped forward and to the side. The crown atop her head clattered to the floor at Elaura's feet.

Elaura looked from the body to the knife in her hand and back again, her pulse roaring in her ears, her mouth open in disbelief. Tears fells in thin streams down her cheeks, tears she had never shed. Sobs shook her body as she mourned the loss of her childhood, the humans her mother's kind had slaughtered, the women who'd died under their rule. Countless lives lay at the feet of the Queens.

Orin came to stand with her, his hand slipping the knife from her fingers and tucking it into his waistband. He bent to pick up the crown, wiping a speck of blood from the crystals. Straightening, he held the crown in both hands and presented it to Elaura.

She didn't look at it, or him. When she spoke, her voice sounded hollow and faraway.

"Did anyone survive?" she asked.

"The Queens are dead. Most of the daughters are

dead or in hiding, the Nurses scattered," he answered.

She nodded, her eyes still trained on the carnage at her feet.

"They're asking for you," he said gently.

"Why me?" she asked. She was no one special, truly.

"You're the Queen now."

"What do I do?"

"Be a good one."

15

Orin was wrong. One Queen and a handful of her consorts survived, though it was not for long. When the chaos of the attack died down and the rebel leaders restored order, they moved the survivors to the courtyard for a makeshift trial. It was mostly symbolic, a way for the newly free people to satisfy their bloodlust and for sympathizers to see exactly who had lost and who now held the power. They were sentenced to death for their crimes, and people from the cities and the camps alike stood in witness as their sentence was carried out. They cheered when their heads rolled from their bodies, but Elaura found no comfort in their deaths.

As she stood on a makeshift podium on the ground where so much blood had been spilled, she could find no comfort in any of it. Nothing would replace the lives that the Queens' quest for absolute power and adulation had destroyed. Nothing would give the broken women of this world back the years they had lost.

She took a deep breath, her fingers worrying at the folds of her dress. She still wore it in the same draping style as before, but she'd requested one made of fabric red as blood, a symbol of the blood spilled and the cost of their freedom. Over it, she wore a thick cloak clasped at her neck. It fit smartly at her shoulders, draping down her back and split open at the front. Upon her head was the crown of her mother, heavy in more than just its weight. She was determined that it would be a symbol of unity, a circle representing equality and balance.

Elaura didn't know if she deserved to rule, but the rebel leaders seemed to think it was the best choice. She was the *People's Queen*, she thought sardonically. It was ironic they should so vehemently support her, considering how easily they'd been prepared to let her die. There would be a formal vote, of course, and as their world rebuilt and the local populations nominated leaders into their respective positions, they would form a newly created Parliament. For now, these people before her, people whose numbers filled the courtyard and stretched down every street as far as her eye could see, needed to know that the powers that governed them during this transition were trustworthy. They needed to hear her words again, words she'd never known held this much power.

"You're the woman who broke the system from the inside. Your words stoked the fires of a revolution," Gabriel said, leaning forward from the line of her husbands behind her to whisper into her ear. Talyn and Orin nodded in support. "Now they'll keep the future burning bright."

Elaura smiled at him and took a steadying breath. She stepped up to the podium, her hands clasped tightly before her.

"We stand here on the very ground where they stole our freedoms away from us. Through lies and trickery and manipulation, with fear and desperation, they whittled away at us. It is the same ground where we fought to take it back. No longer will we be sacrificed to serve the needs of those who would harm us. No longer will we be punished, chained, tortured, or sent to be slaves to an alien master. From now until the end of our days, we live free to work together in unity, to pursue our health, our happiness..."

She looked back at the three men standing at her back, the husbands she never expected to love or be loved by, and her heart filled.

"And to love who we choose."

ABOUT THE AUTHOR

Selena Collins is a romance author who likes her characters strong and her happily ever afters spicy. Her work often includes the fantastical, dark, macabre, or paranormal, making for sensual stories with a dash of "other."

She lives outside of Atlanta, Georgia with her children and their zoo of pets. In her spare time, she makes silly videos on the internet, takes all of her hobbies to 11, and reads voraciously.

To go behind the scenes, stalk her social media (in a non-creepy way, of course), or read more books by Selena, visit selenacollins.com.